Instrument of Death

Thomas J. Ault

Copyright © 2012 Author Name

All rights reserved.

ISBN: 1974291057
ISBN-13: 9781974291052

ACKNOWLEDGMENTS

To the wonderful people who read the
Deavereau Series of Detective Mysteries.

and

To my patient and understanding wife who
puts up with me during the hours
spent on the writing and research of the books.

and

To my friend and mentor, Marshall Frank
who continues to write best-selling books,
both fiction and non-fiction.

A Fictional Story. Any resemblance to Characters, Names, Places, or Incidents is Purely Coincidental.

Original Copyright June 2017

PROLOGUE

Barry was an unsuspecting victim whose uncle left him a valuable instrument. What he didn't know was it was also left to someone else who wanted it more than he did.

Sean, a collector, became a person of interest in the search for the lost instrument, even though that didn't appear to be his original plan.

No one expected murder while Deavereau and Lori pushed to solve the case, but as greed took hold, desperate measures were needed!

Some families become devious when money is involved, and Gertrude Dono became more vicious that most. The Dono family loved money, and their ideas of fairness were lost long before Deavereau got involved. Aunt Gertrude's daughter and son discovered the outside world was incompatible with their mother's plans for their future.

Lori, Deavereau's beautiful and talented partner, becomes a true investigator, working alongside her mentor, Bill Deavereau, while chasing the misfits in this investigation called the "Instrument of Death."

Instrument of Death

CHAPTER 1

I heard someone moving around the outer office and raised up from my chair, removed my .45 from my desk drawer and slipped across the room to open the door a crack. The reception area was too dark for me to see clearly, so I opened the door a bit further. There was a figure in the darkness! Suddenly a beam of light ripped into my eyes like an ice pick so I raised my left hand to shade them.

The whispery voice of a woman emanated from the darkness.

I wiped the sleep from my eyes. "Good lord Lori, what are you doing here at this ungodly hour? Why the flashlight? What time is it anyhow?"

Lori shot back, "I couldn't sleep, that reception area lightbulb you were going to replace didn't get replaced, and it is almost 5:30 in the morning! The real question is, what are you doing here?"

"I fell asleep while studying an old case!"

My excuse for being there didn't fly so I told the truth.

"My landlady kicked me out."

Lori was less than gracious! "Kicked you out? Why?"

I told her that the landlady didn't like my occasional cigar, or me, for that matter, and she said something about my rent. That lit Lori's fuse. "Bill, I told you to quit smoking in the apartment. She told you it is a "non-smoking" place now. What is there about her new rules that you don't get?" She took a breath and then continued with her questioning, "And why haven't you paid your rent?"

I tried to make excuses, but nothing I said was what Lori wanted to hear. She looked at me with that disgusted look she gets when she thinks I've done something stupid. There wasn't any sense in continuing the conversation. It would only get worse, so I left the question about rent hanging. I half growled at her in an attempt to change the subject, suggesting that since she ruined my sleep, the least she could do was put on the coffee.

Lori's scowl remained, and with an indignant response, she answered, "Do I look like your maid? I'm your partner, or have you forgotten that." She walked to the sink and filled the coffee urn. While the pot was filling, she looked across the room at me. "You didn't answer me about the rent!"

I still didn't answer. I wouldn't give her the satisfaction of thinking she had won the scrimmage. I retreated to my office bathroom and turned on the water to shave. Needing to have the last word, she shouted, to overcome the sound of the water, "When you're done, clean it up in there, 'cause I'm not going to clean up after you, I have enough to take care of."

Even with her bossiness, times were good. She enjoyed reminding me to do things, like pay my rent, keep the office neat, and other stuff that she thought I need reminded of. She became a bit pushier since she got her own P.I. license and I made her my partner, but I wouldn't want her any other way! She's young and aggressive, and bright as the sun. I hate to admit it, but I needed someone to give me a shove from time to time!

I finished shaving while the coffee brewed. Admittedly it wasn't the strong stuff I made, but it was drinkable. One time, she took a sip of my brew and nearly choked. I liked mine stronger, but as time went by, hers seemed easier to swallow.

She shouted from the office area, "Hurry up, we don't have all day, your coffee is going to get cold!" She didn't need to yell. I heard the coffee stop brewing, and I mentioned that she was the one who came in so darn early, so now she had to wait for me! I needed my caffeine boost.

She retaliated. "Really? How long five minutes, ten minutes, maybe an hour. Are you having to apply make-up or what? Like I said, we don't have all day!"

I spread some deodorant in my armpits, pulled on a fresh shirt, and tucked it into my trousers, all the time wishing that the day could have gotten along without me.

She continued with her bossy attitude. "Hurry up! Come in here and drink this cup of coffee!" I asked her what was so important.

She started talking as soon as I sat down.

"Remember, last year, you had a client who turned out to be a crook, remember him?"

Jokingly I answered, "Which one?"

Of course I remembered him! Who could forget the guy with a fake accent and the insane name of Benjamin Franklin Spears? It was his group of idiots that gave me gray hair way before my time!

Lori gave me that disgusted look, knowing I was baiting her with a little humor. She paid no attention to my joke and went on to tell me that the case kept her awake. I knew there was something reminiscent about the new case, but I couldn't put my finger on it. Then it bursted into my memory like a thunder bolt! Spears hired us to find that old clock, but discovering what it was actually worth, we realized that he was really after a gold statue.

She took a sip of her coffee, then continued that this new client also wanted us to find something unusual. He contacted us just like Spears pretending to be some aristocrat did, but instead inferred that he was a banker.

I'm wasn't sure what she meant. She was right that he didn't come on like a rich aristocrat. He did say he worked at a bank and he did have a strange request.

She asked if I realized that he knew I had used unorthodox methods in the past. The fact that O'Hara mentioned the counterfeit money plates I found for Oliver Best, the F.B.I. agent meant that he had to do some undercover work on his own to know that. She was right in questioning where he could have found that out.

I understood what she was leading up to when she said that she thought O'Hara had knowledge about the old case and was trying to use similar tactics to get us to do something devious!

There have been several occasions people chose the 'old me' for things I did before Lori got involved. A buck was a buck back then, and I didn't always care how I got it. It was tough getting the agency started.

I understood what she was getting at, but I didn't agree with her completely, so I suggested that we drag the old white board out and make some notes.

Lori smiled (finally), and agreed with me. She got the board and sharpies out while I finished my coffee.

CHAPTER 2

I held the cup of coffee between my hands. The warmth of the cup felt good. I was ready to work. Lori asked where I thought we should start. Still feeling jovial, I suggested that we start with his name. Lori gave me a disgusted look, but started with that... and few other things she could remember.

1. Name: Sean O'Hara. - Irish decent.
2. Works at Brown National Bank.-Cashier
3. Single- has no family,
4. Home address, 1600 Willow, Apartment 2, Albertville."

Having completed the obvious, she glared at me across the desk, and asked what was next.

I suggested we should write down what he wanted us to find. She wrote:

5. Computer Search: FDR's missing P/R check-March 1936-
6. Reason for choosing us: Found counterfeit plates for Oliver Best

Lori suggested we should learn more about this guy before we got too involved, just to make sure that everything was on the 'up and up.' I agreed, and decided that while she was checking out Sean, I would start on the grunt work searching the computer for that check to "FDR."

Lori treaded softly, foolishly thinking she might hurt my feelings by suggesting that she should handle the computer stuff and I should start the physical search. I gave her my quickie smile and agreed. Her skills on the computer were better than mine, and there was that possibility there could be some "tough guy" requirements that would need to be addressed.

Lori, looked up from her laptop and motioned that there was more coffee, but I passed on the invitation, deciding that time was of the essence. Getting information on O'Hara shouldn't be too hard. His bank was local, and it's been there for an eternity. His history should have been just a matter of a phone call to establish his current employment...this should have been a piece of cake!

I read the file Lori left on my desk regarding our Mr. O'Hara. I considered we might have taken this case just because we needed a client, but the wrong clientele could be bad for our business! I pulled my recorder from the desk drawer and set it to rewind. I hoped that the recording of our original conversation would refresh my memory of what was said. It purred like a newborn kitten as it rewound. When it finished, I set it to play, and adjusted the volume.

"Mr. Deavereau, my name is Sean O'Hara. I understand that you find things for people."

"It depends on what you are were looking for."

"I'm looking for a rather unusual thing. A check."

"A check?"

"Yes, a check, but not just any check, but a check made out to President Franklin D. Roosevelt sometime in the 1930's or early 40's."

"What is so important about that check?"

"Only four have been found. I am a collector of FDR's memorabilia and would like to add one of those to his collection."

"Are you aware of the cost to find something like that?"

"No, I am not. What are your rates?"

"We charge $500.00 per day plus expenses and a retainer of $1000.00. Expenses can run from nothing to a hundred or more a day, depending on what we might run into."

"That is bit more than I had anticipated. Can you do it any cheaper?"

"Unfortunately no. I have the office, the partner, gas, car upkeep, insurance, and a lot more things to pay for and we just can't work for any less. You might find us expensive, but if you compare us to other detective agencies..."

"Will the retainer be refunded?"

"Yes, provided you pay our billing upon receipt."

"I understand. I should have known since I deal with business accounts on a daily basis. Will you take a check?"

"Yes."

"Here is a check, will you need any more money now?"

"No, that is enough. We bill weekly and give a complete accounting of the expenses, if there are any."

"I see. How soon can you start?"

"Tomorrow, the sooner we start, the sooner you will have that special check."

The recorder clicked off. It has saved me more times than I would care to admit.

I removed the cell phone from my shirt pocket, and hit the contact icon. Up popped the number I wanted. The phone rang twice and a lovely voice answered; "Brown National Bank, we value your business. All of our associates are busy with a customer or have stepped away from their desks. We ask that you please dial "1" for New Accounts, dial "2" for Existing Accounts, dial "3" for Credit Card information, dial "4" for Your Bank Balance, or dial "5" for our Staff Registry; if none of these are what you are seeking please stay on line or dial "0" for the operator."

This makes me want to bang down the receiver on some hard surface, but that won't work with a cell phone; I think I'll just hang up; how stupid, that would be foolish since nothing would be accomplished; I know, why not dial "0" and complain? These ideas aren't going to work! Just push "5" to find the guy I want.

The registry showed Jack Falcone's extension was 243. I selected it only to discover that the bank would not open until 9:00 A.M. and it was only 8. Lori, awakening me at around 5:30 that morning, made me start work much earlier than I was accustomed to, and it was taking its toll on me.

Since it was too early to reach anyone at the bank, I asked Lori how she was doing with her computer [playing]. I chuckled at my little joke, but Lori didn't respond. She was deep into something that was probably over my head, so I took out a cigar that was given me by a friend of mine.

I was about to light it, when she suddenly acknowledged my question telling me she wasn't playing. She continued admonishing me about my cigar suggesting a good place for it would be in the toilet.

That had to be the fastest reaction ever to my lighting up! I decided to take a walk. I wandered down the hall to the front door and stepped out into the 72-degree morning sunshine and the weather of fall.

What a glorious day it was. The sun was shining, birds were singing from the treetops. A few white clouds were in the sky, and a slow breeze wound its way through my thinning hair.

I lit my cigar, and walked to the bus stop bench next to the office park garage. My mind was finally clear and life was great...well almost great. The idea that I had to find a new apartment ruined things being totally great!

Suddenly Lori appeared at the entrance of our office building and called to me, saying that she had found something and I needed to look at it. Then, as an afterthought, she told me to get rid of that horrible smelling cigar!

Lori interrupted my commune with nature and ruined my fine cigar moment with her comment. Now I had to throw my cigar away, return to the stuffy air space of the office, and get back to work...darn! I should have taken a longer walk.

Lori was sitting straight in her side chair, both feet on the chair rung, with her knees raised above where they would normally be, allowing the laptop to precariously balance there. I don't know why she didn't go into her own office and use the big computer on her desk.

If I ever reach a point that I understand women, I'll probably be close to leaving this earth for a better place!

I asked her what was so important and she told me that she found that of all the checks FDR received, there were only four found. It didn't mention which checks were found, other than the first one. She said she was curious as to why Sean would want just one of them? They were ancient, and with not a lot of value, except to a museum, or the National Archives in DC. She decided $8,500.00 for one he sought wasn't too bad, and stopped talking. Using her left shoe, she gently massaged her right ankle, like she always does when she's concentrating.

I waited, knowing something was coming. She told me there had to be a reason he wanted it, and when she got the info she was looking for about him, she would find the answer.

It seemed like a lot of time had passed and the bank still wasn't open...actually not quite an hour. Time passes slowly when you are waiting. Maybe I could do something while I'm waiting, like count the minutes?

I drummed my fingers on my desktop, walked around my desk a few times, and stood looking over Lori's shoulder, numerous times. Finally 9:00 AM came. It was time to place the call to the bank! I listened to their options, controlled my temper, and finally I got to Option #5. I selected extension number 243 for Jack Falcone, and he answered, including his department's name.

I told him who I was, and asked how he was on such a fine day. It took a second or two before he answered my greeting and told me he was doing fine. He asked how I was so I told him I was well. I added a little more small talk inquiring how his golf game was doing. I knew he played and hoped a personal touch might make it easier for me to get the background information I needed.

He answered that his game had improved and that he had shot an 87 the day before. I told him I hadn't played lately, too busy. I gave him that old adage about 'idle hands.' Feeling I had spent enough time smoozing, I reminded him that I ran the Deavereau Detective Agency and needed to check on a prospective client that works at his bank. I gave him Sean O'Hara's name and address.

Jack was hesitant to give me the information so I advised him again that O'Hara was a prospective client.

He told me he wanted to keep things on the up and up and told me that I should know how tight security was regarding private information, and that they were limited on what they could divulge, especially since every phone call was recorded. I told him that I understood and also had certain guidelines to follow.

He put me on hold a few minutes while he found the information. It seemed like another hour went by, but it was only a few minutes before Falcone came back on the phone.

He asked me if I had a pencil and I told him that I did, then he read from the employment record:

Name: Sean Michael O'Hara

Age: 28

Marital Status: Single

Employment Date: September 3, 2014.

Address: 1600 Willow, Apartment 2, Albertville, Alabama.

Education: Graduate of Ole Miss in 2010.

I asked if there was anything about the subjects he took at Ole Miss, or anything else that might be pertinent and he replied that O'Hara graduated with a degree in accounting, and a minor in history. His work record was confidential, but he did tell me that they did a complete background check, as they always did on new employees, and he passed.

I knew he was limited in what he could tell me, but at least I had something to start on. I thanked him for his help. He asked if there was anything else that he could help me with and I told him "No, but thank you," and closed out the call. It was time to call Detective Johnson at the police station, and see what information I could get from him.

Lori asked me if I learned anything of interest on O'Hara and I gave her the information to enter on our white board, then I picked up my cell and pushed the speed dial for the police department. She continued talking, explaining that she that she had located the check using her computer. It wasn't in hiding, and as a matter of fact was far from it. There was a dealer in Huntsville who had the check, had posted it for sale at $500.00, apparently not knowing the real value, and hoping for a "quick sale."

My thoughts were interrupted when a pleasant receptionist brightened my day with, "Good morning, Guntersville Police Station," and asked how she could direct my call. I asked her to transfer me to Detective Johnson and she did. I knew he was going to try and sideline me with a lot of red tape. He's that kind of "by the book" cop.

Maybe, if I approach him as my friend, I can bypass the crap and get the information I need.

I asked him how his fishing trip worked out, and he told me it was lousy. Deciding the friend approach wasn't the best way to go, I asked him if the name Sean O'Hara sounded familiar, and if it did, was there anything I should be concerned about. As I suspected, he started in on me as soon as I popped the question about O'Hara. He told me that without the paper work, I wasn't going to get any information, friend of not!

I gave him O'Hara's name again, and started to give him the address, when he interrupted and asked if Will and I were working the same client. I told him I didn't think so, and asked him why? Disgustedly, he told me that I should know how he felt about wasting his time! I was startled with that response, told him thanks for nothing, and hit the off button on my phone.

Lori asked me what Johnson had to say. I told her that it appeared our friends, Will and Linda, had inquired about this guy yesterday, and that was all Johnson would tell me, other than to quit wasting his time. Knowing I was ticked off at his lack of giving us any information, she asked me, what spur got under his saddle. I told her that I had no idea, but he'd just have to get over it.

We decided to see our friends and find out why they were looking into the background of this new client of ours. I finished my coffee, pushed the whiteboard back into the closet, so no one could see it, and then we left for Will's office.

CHAPTER 3

What a great place to live. Sadly there were some bad memories from the past. I can still remember the car careening down the cliff, Will and the others, tethered to their chairs inside this home when it was a hunting cabin. I am so glad that incident with the Napoleon clock is behind us. I can't forget how Will's first partner, the unscrupulous John Cunningham, was sent to prison for his masterminding Mr. Spears and his ring of thieves. Linda was Will's secretary since he first opened his office a little over a year ago, then they became partners, not only in the collection agency in Guntersville, but later in love and marriage. They have developed a good business, dealing with several of the locals, as well as the banks.
They changed the old cabin into this beautiful home on Nigro Mountain, added a bit more land to their acreage, (which included the old cottage, originally owned by the wealthy Jacobin family from Tampa, Florida, and now a guest house) and they are still building for their future.

The day was just beginning on Nigro Mountain. The sun was shining, just enough to reflect the light off one of the many bluffs overlooking Lake Guntersville. A squirrel jumped around the concrete parking area with a nut in its mouth while birds sang their songs of cheer.

Will and his wife, Linda had just arisen.

"Hon, have you seen my razor? I thought I left it here on the sink."

"Not since last night when I used it to shave my legs."

Agitated, Will looked at the end of the tub, next to the faucets, and found his razor there. He knew it was going to cut his face the minute he tried to shave because he had forgotten to buy new blades when he was at the drugstore the day before. There was no way he could replace the dull one!

"Dawgonit sweetheart, you know that when you shave those beautiful legs of yours, it ruins my razor blade, and I get cuts all over my face."

Linda edged into the bathroom a bit, just far enough to kiss Will on the cheek, touch his face with her finger, and tell him, "You even look cute with those little pieces of paper stuck on those cuts."

"Alright now, you're taking advantage of my good nature." Will smiled and continued his morning preparations.

After a few years of being married to an angel, how

could he feel any way but lucky to have her?

As Will was getting dressed, he said, "Linda, I got a phone call yesterday, from Deavereau." Then he asked, "Did I tell you about it?"

Linda stepped back from the door, as Will, (with a few small patches of facial tissue adorning his face), came out of the bathroom for breakfast. "No, you didn't. What did he have to say? Anything important?"

Will made his way to the chair in their breakfast nook and looked out of the window overlooking the concrete parking area. (He had built it for their cars a year before.) He watched as a hawk swooped down on its prey and the other birds in the area scurried away, flying to safety.

He answered her, "It wasn't anything earth shaking. Deavereau was starting a new case and thought I might have some knowledge about the object he was seeking. Why, I don't have the slightest idea, since we don't get involved in his kind of investigation work."

Linda always was a step ahead of Will when it came to handling the simple things. That was what made their agency special.

"Tell me what he wanted, maybe I have an idea or two. Remember we are partners." She looked across the table at him with her mischievous smile.

"Yeah, you do get more involved in our archives than I do." Now it was his turn to smile with that devilish look, but in a joking way.

"Well, tell me." Linda responded as she poured the coffee. "It must have been interesting or you wouldn't have brought it up."

Sheepishly, Will answered her question. "You know me too well."

She smiled. "Yes I do, and you better not forget it."

"Well, it seems like some guy wants him to find a lost check."

Linda leaned on her elbows as she sipped her coffee, and then answered, "That sounds like something we might do if we were searching for a forger."

"Well," Will took a drink of his coffee, "this check is a few years old, and belongs to either the government, or the heirs of President Franklin Delano Roosevelt."

"What?" Linda wasn't sure she heard him right.

"That's what I said. He's looking for a check that was given to the president back in the 1930's, or maybe the 40's."

Linda hearing what he said, again asked, "What in the world for?"

"I have no idea hon, no idea at all. Some of these people that Bill runs into seem to be a card short of a deck."

The smile left her face as Linda responded with, "I hate to admit it, but I think you're right about that." Then thinking about that, she continued, "Wasn't it a year or so ago that they were looking for a clock, and it turned out to be a statue that the guy was really looking for?"

Will smiled. "Yes, that was a wild case. It even cost me my partner in the diving business, but look at the partner I have now!"

An adorable whimper came from the new addition that they had added to the cottage…a sound of joy, an infant's cry.

"Oh, oh! We just awakened Julia. Hold that thought while I tend to her, okay?"

Will took another sip of his coffee and stared out of the window and to watch more of nature's day unfold. He thought back to how he and his partner, then in the diving recovery business, had decided on this location, built the original cottage, board by board. He reminisced about how they found the place so enticing and the perfect deer hunting spot

Linda returned, with Julia in her arms. "You don't think Bill wants you to get involved do you?"

"Hon, he's hoping that we might have some tidbit of information for him. He probably thinks that since we are in the business of bill collecting, strange checks might not be too far out of our reach as well."

"I hope you are right…, he knows that you don't handle his type of investigation." Linda was concerned that they might become involved in another case like that one last year, and it wasn't a pleasant feeling.

"They are friends you know. Even if we don't see them often, as fellow detectives we do, from time to time, give a little help to each other."

Will knew that while she still enjoyed our

friendship, she was not keen on getting involved with any dangerous case like the one last year.

"Are you ready to leave for the office yet, or are you going in, since the baby sitter is off for a few days?"

Will was hoping that Linda, with Julia in her arms, would consider going with him. He had made a place for little Julia at the office for those times when they could take her with them.

Linda placed Julia in Wills arms. "Here, you take Julia, let me turn off the coffee maker and put the cups into the washer, then I'll go with.

CHAPTER 4

The drive to Will's office was less than five minutes. We arrived there as they were unlocking the front door. He saw us and remarked to his wife, "Look whose coming calling so early in the morning," then asked us to what did they owe this pleasure to.

He was almost too much to handle so early in the morning, with that handsome smile of his,

I answered that we had been working since around six that morning, and needed a search made for a guy named Sean O'Hara.

Will, opened the door for his wife and daughter and made a suggestion to Linda that it sounded to him like they were going to have company for a while and suggested she put on some coffee. She agreed, and handed the baby over to Will to put in the "Baby Tenda." (It was one that we had found for them last year in Joanne's old store building.)

We followed Will and Linda into the inner office and sat down. While Linda started the coffee. Will sat down and fidgeted with some things on his desk. He finally raised his eyes to meet ours and asked how we had come into contact with Sean.

I explained Sean's approach to us and the conversation with Johnson. I repeated Johnson's question as to why we were both working the same client. Then I asked why he was investigating O'Hara, was it personal or business.

Sean sat back in his chair and told us that it wouldn't hurt anything if he told us that they had a client that thinks O'Hara owed him a lot of money. Money that was allegedly loaned to him over a year or so ago. There wasn't much information to go on, so he decided to run a background check on him. He said that he filled out all the paperwork and took it to Johnson, and yesterday he received the information needed to complete his inquiry.

I figured it had to be something like that, but I still needed more information, so I asked Will if he got enough information to either clear Sean, or indict him. He told me they were still working on the case. It was a muddy mess and he couldn't tell us everything, due to client privilege, but he could can tell us that either this O'Hara was a nutcase, or... he was slicker than leather soles on sawdust.

Lori and I looked at each other. We both had a sinking feeling that our client could not be trusted. I felt it was my turn for transparency, so I explained that after the weirdo case last year that involved the gold statue, the Napoleon Clock, his partner, and all the other craziness, we had been taking deeper looks into our clients before we got involved. We felt this O'Hara guy's request was strange so we were checking him out.

We stopped the conversation when Linda came

back into the room with a fresh pot of coffee. There wasn't much more to talk about, so we sat back and enjoyed the coffee. Breaking the ice to talk about something, other than business, was Lori's job, but for some reason or other, I asked if they would like to join us for dinner. Will took advantage of the invitation, reminding us that a few weeks ago, I told him that we owed them, and should consider dinner the next evening, at the Rock House.

Lori interrupted saying that she was glad Will remembered that since we had decided, on our way over, that it was time to act on that invitation. I felt like the cat caught with a goldfish in its mouth.

There was a slight hesitation when Will, in a questioning way, looked at Linda. She nodded in agreement to his unspoken question. He, knowing our business hadn't been going as well as it could have, suggested we go dutch-treat. I answered not this time, the treat was on us.

Twice they have been a great help to us, and though we have needed them from time to time, they have never needed us, but I hoped that they might in the future.

Will answered me with, okay, the Rock House it is, and then asked what time would we like them to meet us. Lori, looking directly at Linda, suggested that since they (the girls) had to look just right, we should make it a later, rather than an earlier dinner, and thought eight o'clock would be fine.

Linda, glanced questionably at Will, and then looking directly at Lori told her that as long as their baby sitter was available, that would be a perfect time. Then she added that Lori didn't need any extra time to look beautiful. Motherhood hadn't dropped in on her, yet.

Taken by surprise, Lori, with an embarrassed shade of pink overtaking her normally perfect complexion, answered that she really would need extra time and that she couldn't understand how Linda could manage to be so perfect, after having a beautiful child to take care of, working, and taking care of their home.

Thank goodness the flowery talk between them ended. I suggested that Lori and I had a lot of work to get done before we could start getting ready for the evening and asked them to give us a call, if there was a baby sitter problem.

CHAPTER 5

Knock, knock!
I yelled through the door saying that whoever was there should come on in instead of knocking.

Why people didn't just come in was beyond me! The door was never locked, and it said quite plainly on the sign, "Deavereau Detective Agency" and "Enter."

A poorly dressed fellow with a ponytail, an earring in his left ear, and a pockmarked face came through the door. Generally this type of person is looking for a free handout, potential clients are generally more affluent looking. I stood up, extended my hand, asked what his name was, and what we could do for him.

He answered that his name was Barry Dono. He was a bit hesitant, almost appearing embarrassed as he sat down and took out a pack of cigarettes.

Lori entered the front office and saw what he was about to do. She didn't hesitate a bit to tell him this was a non-smoking office!

I assume that his appearance probably had something to do with her abruptness. He apologized and told us that wouldn't happen again.

He complied with our office rules of smoking etiquette, but he couldn't do much for his current dress styles. He looked to be right out of the '60s.

Was he a late blooming flowerchild?

I told him to relax, and that I, from time to time, had a cigar. I cupped my hand around my mouth, hoping that Lori couldn't hear me, and whispered that when I tried smoking in the office, I got the same treatment from Lori. After hearing that, he seemed more at ease. I introduced Lori as my partner and then he understood.

Concerned that we wouldn't help him, he told us he didn't have a lot of bucks, but he needed some help, and asked if we did all kinds of detective stuff. I looked at Lori and saw her blank expression. We had never had a client like him before, and neither of us could imagine his being in search of anything valuable. I explained that we search for old things people want us to find. I was concerned that the word 'antique' might be over his head. I assumed, incorrectly!

In his hesitating style of speech, he told us that he was the black sheep of the Dono family. He indicated that we had probably never heard of them since they made their bucks in investments, they seldom made the papers, and didn't want to. They didn't run in the high society groups, and lastly, they didn't live in a fancy district of town.

After another hesitation, he explained that all

they did was enjoy the fruits of the good investments his Uncle John had made, and then they hoarded the money. That answered part of the question we both had, with respect to his background, and it possibly answered whether he could afford us. I asked him to continue.

He looked away from our searching eyes momentarily, and told us that his Uncle John had recently passed away. We told him that we were sorry to hear that, and asked if he had been ill for some time. We felt it necessary to be consoling at this point.

He said it was rather sudden, a heart attack. Then, looking directly into my eyes, he told us he wasn't interested in a will or that "stuff."

All he wanted was what his uncle told him he was leaving him, in the event of his death.

Lori was curious and asked what that might be, and did he to receive it?

Barry stared at the floor before raising his eyes to meet Lori's, then answered her that there were two instruments. a banjo and a mandolin, and no, he didn't receive them.

Why would anyone want to hire us to locate two old instruments?

He smiled a quick smile that faded back into his non-expression. He told us that he could see, by the look on our faces, that we were questioning his sanity.

Glancing at Lori, then back at me, he confessed that he was a musician that didn't make a lot of money by playing the guitar and singing, but he did get by. The mandolin and banjo player was his Uncle John. He played a 1920 Gibson Mandolin and a very special Banjo. With his continual hesitation style of speech, he told us that the Mandolin was roughly worth $30,000.00, and the banjo around $22,000.00. He continued telling us that not only were they pricey, but that they were wonderful instruments to play. He told us that all stringed instruments...are not equal.

We understood his desire to get them, especially since they were left to him, and asked why the family didn't honor his uncle's wishes. We had no idea of their true value, but it was obvious that was the reason for wanting to hire us.

Lori asked if, in other words, he wanted to both own and play them. He responded with a "Yes mam," and told us the mandolin had a very soft, string touch ferret-board, making it easier to play than most mandolins. The banjo not only was also easy playing and had the same fingering, but perfect for what he did.

He explained that he played a lot of 40's and 50's music, which prompted Lori to tell him that was very interesting but she assumed he would prefer the new stuff, like rock and rap.

He told her she was right about that, but since he performed at festivals, a few weddings, some class reunions, and other places of that type, where older folks attended, what he performed was the only way to go. He was so soft spoken, the caverns in his complexion seemed to fade away. Removing the earring and the ponytail from our minds, we saw a quiet, sophisticated young man who was a professional, and had a reasonable request. His speech hesitation did seem unusual for an entertainer

Our real concern, was still his ability to pay us, so Lori, contemplating a "no" answer, told Barry that she understood his needs, but wondered if he could afford us. She continued that our rates were $500.00 per day, plus expenses, and a $1,000.00 retainer.

I thought she was too abrupt because the guy had a legitimate reason for needing us, and I wanted to help him. Of course, once we drop our requirements, it could continue, so I quickly overcame my sympathy pang.

He told Lori that he had been putting away money after each gig and he had also sold a couple of his outdated sound equipment pieces. He said he would be fine as long as we didn't expect to go over $10,000.00, and asked if that sounded possible.

Lori changed her tune, realizing he had a lot more than she thought he did, and asked exactly what he wanted us to do. He said he wasn't sure. He knew that we couldn't steal them, but assumed that we would somehow retrieve them for him, since his Uncle John told him they would be his someday.

Lori suggested that Barry let us discuss it and get back to him the following day. He leaned on the reception desk and told me he could wait, but if we decided earlier he would like to know. I stood and extended my hand to him and told him we would do that. At that point he asked us to call him Barry, instead of the 'Mr. Dono' thing. I assured him we would do that, telling him it would be easier for us as well.

Barry stood, dropped his business card on my desk, turned, and walked to the door. As he left, he told me next time he would read the sign and just come in without knocking.

CHAPTER 6

The morning came, too early as usual, and I was sleeping in the office when Lori arrived. She awakened me asking if I had found a new apartment yet. Sleepily, I raised up from the couch, and told her that I didn't, and for right now I was quite happy where I was.

She told me that she could see that I thought this was my bedroom, but, it was not, that this was our office, not a flophouse!

I tried to be agreeable, or at least I thought I did when I told her she was right!

She shocked me into reality when she told me we were going apartment hunting and if I thought for a minute she was going to tolerate my sleeping on that couch, looking scruffy because I didn't shower or hang up my clothes... I had another think coming!

Having nothing else to say, she suggested breakfast, around the corner at the greasy spoon. A couple of eggs sounded good to me but I could hardly believe that she suggested it. She never ate breakfast, she despised that little "greasy spoon" around the corner, and she, eating breakfast with me? That was strange.

As soon as we finished breakfast, she ushered me to my car and forced me to drive to what appeared to be a new place called the "Willows Apartments." It was sharp looking with an entrance that housed several post boxes mounted into the wall. One for each apartment. We pushed the button next to the "MANAGER" brass plate. The manager answered and Lori told her that I was looking for an apartment.

She understood and released the door, then introduced herself as Mrs. McNeil and told us that she and her husband owned the apartment building.

I told her my name was Bill Deavereau and introduced Lori as my associate and partner. She said that she understood and asked if we were looking for something with two bedrooms. I realized what she was thinking and corrected her, explaining, that Lori was a friend, and my business partner.

She asked what kind of business that might be and Lori answered that we were partners in an upper class detective agency. She looked a bit unnerved hearing what we did, and asked if that meant that we would have weapons there… in their place. Then she stopped and told us she didn't think I would fit in very well. Lori tried to save the day stressing that we weren't the kind of people like those that she 'saw on television.'

Mrs. McNeil answered with the old maxim, "You can't tell a book by its cover." She told us that she was sorry for not feeling that we would fit in, but they try to keep their place quiet. She mentioned all of that hullabaloo that took place a year or so ago when their police department got involved in an episode on the lake. She would be concerned that something like that could happen there.

Lori told Mrs. McNeil, that after all was said and done, her home, as well as, her apartment building, belonged to her and her husband and that they had all the right in the world to pick and choose who their tenants might be, then she told her that we were sorry she felt the way she did because I would have been a good tenant.

We returned to my car and drove on to the next apartment. It didn't look like much on the outside. It wasn't falling apart, but it looked like it could use a bath, or a makeover of some kind. We knocked on the door and a man answered. He was shaved, but stubble was starting to show on his face. His shoes appeared to have lost their shine, and his pants had a double crease in them indicating he did his own ironing and wouldn't use a drycleaner. He liked a cigar occasionally, his breath told that story. He was abrupt when he asked if we wanted to look at the apartment

I held out my hand to shake his, and introduced myself and Lori, my associate. He said to come on in, then he winked at Lori ,and continued to say that he got that explanation a lot from guys that came to look... with their girlfriends. Lori wasn't thrilled!

We followed him into the group room. There were chairs around a coffee table in the middle of the room with a couch on the side that faced a nice 50-inch flat screen. A couple of poorly dressed guys, sat in the two chairs facing the television.

He opened up Apartment No. 4. and told us that

it was clean and private. The living room had venetian blinds and a large, leather half-round couch with two small chairs facing it. He told us that if I had company, he winked again at Lori, the bathroom was accessible to the living room.

He told me if I made a mess I had to clean it up, or be charged extra if he had to do it. The rent was $500.00 a month plus my own electricity and the rent would be in advance.

I investigated a bit further and asked about a lease. He guffawed and asked if I was kidding, he only did a month to month, so a week's notice was all that was necessary. Lori gave me that eagle eye meaning she didn't approve.

We got back to the office around four that afternoon. I kind of liked the tough guy attitude of the landlord. The apartment was a "man pad" and I thought I had found the place I wanted. However, after Lori pointed out the pitfalls, I thought maybe I was too quick to make a judgement on the place. She didn't like it, and she was probably right with her thoughts that it was a little too "out there" for me.

What if I had Joanne, my last year's "friend with benefits" visit? She wouldn't be too comfortable visiting me there. Lori was right, I needed to have a decent place to hang my hat.

I picked up my cell and pushed in the numbers on the card the landlord gave me. He answered immediately that it was Bob's Place, and it was he, Bob that was speaking. I told him I had just been there with my business partner, Lori and he answered that he couldn't forget me and the chick, and asked when I was comin' aboard.

I explained that I didn't think his place was quite right for me...at this time. He cut me off with a yeah, he got it, and continued crying that he knew we felt that is place wasn't good enough. Before I could say anything else, he told me not to sweat it, he'd survive without me. That convinced me that we would not have made a good match.

I hung up and my memory kicked in. Down by the water, and just west of the road to Nigro Mountain there was a "Vacancy" sign.

That might have been just the right place for me. It was private, was close to the lake, easy access from there to my office, and looked like a nice clean place to live in. The train tracks did run right behind the place, but how often did that old train come through there? I thought maybe I should ask.

I didn't waste another minute. Lori had already gone home so I drove to the place and found the building clearly marked "Manager's Office." A middle-aged gentleman greeted me when I rang the doorbell. He told me his name was Sven Baker, and he asked if I had come to see the vacant apartment.

I shook his hand, then I told him my name and my occupation, not wanting the same reception I had received earlier. He told me he understood what I did, and asked if I knew Will and Linda, the bill collection' people. I answered that I knew them quite well.

He told me they had met because he had a bad tenant a year or so ago, and they were recommended to him as folks that he could trust to collect the rent the fellow owed him. He said that they did a splendid job and at a reasonable price. In one of their conversations, they mentioned that they had a friend, one who was also in the investigation business, should he ever need one, and that was me.

I told him that I was pleased that he knew them and told him that they had a baby not long ago. He said that he talked to Linda last week, and then asked me if I didn't think the little one was wonderful. After a few more compliments on the child, I felt we had had enough small talk, and agreeing with his assessment of the family, asked to see the apartment.

Mr. Baker grabbed some keys from a board next to the front door of his office, came out, and escorted me to the vacant apartment. He opened it up and told me to go ahead and look it over, and asked me to bring the keys back when I was finished looking.

I found it to be a nice clean place. I entered into the living room, with the kitchen and dining area to the left of the door. The bathroom was between the bedrooms making up the rear of the apartment. I liked the quietness of the place, the light colored walls, and the beautiful landscape scene wallpaper on the dining area wall.

The only drawback was that I would have to buy furniture, where the other apartments were furnished. Undoubtedly I could get something much nicer that no one else had used, and the thought of that was refreshing.

I contemplated the cost of furnishing the place to be around a thousand bucks, or maybe two or maybe I could find a nice used furniture place. It wouldn't be new, but it would be better than the furniture in those other apartments. I left, closed the door, and returned the keys.

Mr. Baker asked me what I thought of the place and I told him I liked it, and asked the price. He told me the price was $750.00 per month plus my electricity."

I asked if he had any idea of the electricity cost.

He told me that it had been around $75.00 a month, and added, that was if I didn't get too carried away with the heat and air. He explained that each unit had its own system that could be regulated accordingly.

Asking about the deposit, he responded that normally he charges a deposit equal to the rent, but since I was a friend of a friend, and not some punk he would have to worry about, he would drop that part…just for me.

I knew this was the best I had found. I asked him to hold the apartment for me for a couple of hours because I had friend I'd like to see it, and if she liked it, I would take it!" He agreed, so I walked back to my car, picked up my cell phone, and called Lori.

I explained that I found a nice place in Guntersville that she would like and was wondering if she would like to see it.

Surprised that I found an apartment so late in the day she told me that she would love to see it. I drove to her place and arrived just as she was coming out of the door. I told that her that she would be surprised at what I found. Always the pessimist, when it comes to me, she told me that I was pretty sure of myself, and that she might not like it at all. I told her she should be nice... today.

We both laughed and had small talk about apartments, the two that she had visited with me, new furnishing versus old, and a lot of other stuff that you tend to make small talk about.

I was excited to show her the place as I parked the car in front of the unit I was going to rent. I flashed a smile that made me look like an idiot as I rushed around the car to open the car door for her.

I asked her to stay where she was while I went to the office to get a key from Mr. Baker. She waited till I returned and opened the apartment, and then followed me inside. After looking around, she told me it was very nice, and that she loved it because it was roomy and pleasant, and it had two bedrooms. She went on to tell me that the beautiful landscape mural in the eating area was unique, and finally, she asked me how I found it.

It was my turn to be a little cocky for a change.

I put on my smart aleck smirk and told her that it was just good investigation work, and that with no one pushing me, (meaning her, without saying so) I didn't have a problem.

She came close and gave me a peck on the cheek. She said that was for the nice apartment I found, and without her help, and she decided that I was starting to grow up... after all. (She got her dig in too.) We went outside, closed the door, and walked around the place. The water, the tracks, the whole thing. I knew she was pleased, now that I would not be sleeping at our office any longer.

CHAPTER 7

Two days, two clients. That was unusual for us. Lori and I had to make some decisions. There was no way to handle two searches at the same time. We already found the location of the check that O'Hara wanted us to find, so all he had to do was buy it and pay us.

Lori felt that we should keep one days charges from the retainer and I agreed. We did spend a day checking him out, and locating the check so he didn't need any more assistance.

We contacted Sean O'Hara and told him where he could find the FDR check and that we were sending him a check for $500.00, a one-day investigation charge. He thanked us profusely, and said he was delighted we had found the check, but was embarrassed that he had taken up our time to find something so simple that was located so easily on the computer.

I think he felt more disgusted that he had to give us $500.00 to do something he could have done without our help.

Barry called that afternoon, and Lori answered the phone. I could hear her articulating the agreements over the phone. Without hearing his side of the conversation, it was clear that he was bringing over the $1,000.00

cash retainer, first thing in the morning.

I stepped into the outer office when Lori hung up the phone. She had a cheerful look and said she felt that although the day had been a busy one so far, it had been a profitable one. We could actually afford to take Will and his wife to dinner.

Although it was early, we had cleared what needed to be done. She had more than a couple of hours to shower, and get "gussied up," as she put it. I could pick her up around 7:30 PM. I just wished I was already moved into the new place, but right then, I was pleased that I had this nice office bathroom to use.

CHAPTER 8

We had a lot of information to get from Barry Dono; a description of the instruments, the usual family information, , how many relatives were involved in the inheritance and how close were they, and last but not least, why hire us to find something that appeared so easy to locate himself. All of these things we needed to understand, before we could start.

Lori removed the white-board from the closet and decided to use the corkboard side too, so we could pin pictures on it. We needed a picture of the mandolin and a picture of the banjo.

Suddenly, the door opened, without a knock this time. It was Barry. I stepped into the reception area at the same time Lori did, and we greeted him at the same time. We looked at each other in amazement! Barry's face brightened as he remarked that was like a double whammy! He felt that he was in the right place at the right time and with the right people. We started to speak again at exactly the same time, and all three of us laughed in disbelief.

Maybe we have been working together too long?

I kept quiet and let her tell him that we were glad he was there because in order to start, we needed more information. My recorder turned on, I was ready for our interview. I pulled up a side chair for him and explained that we needed a complete description of the instruments, and some other pertinent information.

Barry complied, using his hesitation style of talking, he told us he would first describe the banjo. He told us it was designed as a special instrument, made sometime during either the 1940's or 1950's. It had a bit longer neck than usual and the entire underside of the instrument had a beautifully designed Indian headdress engraved on it, in color. He told us it also had special lights around the entire body, making it stand out at night when being played. It was a 'one of a kind' instrument.

I motioned to Lori to read what she had written. She read her brief notes and Barry verified that they were accurate. He went on to describe the mandolin and handed us a picture with a written description. He even had a picture of the mandolin case. The description said that it was a 1920 instrument, shipped in 1920 from Gibson. The model was, according to Spurn's Guide to Gibson, a F4 and the Serial Number was 56284. Lori wrote everything down, double checked the information, then pinned the pictures of them both, and the mandolin case to the corkboard. I felt we could locate the banjo with the description of the Indian headdress on the back and with the added lights, but the mandolin would be a different matter.

I suggested that next we talk about his relatives, and asked what he could tell us about them. Barry was reluctant talking about them, until I assured him that whatever he told us, or we wrote on the board, would go no further, and that seemed to satisfy him. He loosened up and told us that his Aunt was still in the large home on the hill. She spent most of her time with a group of snobs that play cards, have tea and that sort of stuff. She was quite dull and a bit snooty. If it had not been for his uncle, she would have nothing except her wickedness! He explained that he didn't know how she could be so different from his uncle. His eyes watered, as he mentioned him, then he continued to tell us that his cousin, Ruth, was much like her mother. She was 22 years old, college educated, but only with a liberal arts degree. She liked to put on airs, from time to time, which were quite discouraging. She had long blond hair, a very pretty face, with a couple of freckles on her nose, and a lovely figure. Then he described her brother, Nathaniel, whom he saw as "a rascal indeed." He had been in and out of trouble for as long as Barry could remember. He was then 26 years old, but without college. He spent four years in the army, never got above the rank of corporal, and ended up frequently in the brig for his temper tantrums. Had it not been for his father, Barry's uncle John, who had been a colonel in the army and a friend of the commanding officer, he probably would have received a dis-honorable discharge. I asked Barry why he said that, and seemingly ashamed, he told us that Nathaniel seemed to have a desire to own everything, and unfortunately that included everything in the barracks, regardless to whom it may have belonged. He stole some things, but his father, being the type of fellow he was, always got such matters resolved without much fanfare or publicity.

    I told him it was a shame, and asked him to repeat the cousin's name, again. Barry had some difficulty with that. He tried to be an honorable person and felt awkward telling us about his cousin's personal life. Finally he answered my request, that the name was Nathaniel. I felt a little guilty about going into his family any further, but at the same time I knew I had to have some information on his uncle. I reassured him that we would act with the utmost caution in our investigation and told him that we had a lot of information on the aunt and the cousins, but no information on his uncle, other than that he seemed to be a nice fellow. Hesitantly, he gave us limited information about his uncle John. He told us that he kept to himself, had several charities that he contributed to, and at least once a week, he disappeared. I asked where he disappeared to. Barry told us that his uncle played with some of his buddies, a couple of times a week. They had a jam session at his closest friend's house. I asked him if he knew the man's name. He answered that he did. I told him to give the information to Lori as we would have to check into him and the others. I reassured him we would not do anything that would involve him in any way. He gave Lori their names, Guy Billings, Billy Joe Rigby, and Tony Schwartz. He only knew Guy's address and gave it to her to write down.

    Lori diligently wrote everything on the whiteboard, including the personal information:

Name: Barry Jonathan Dono,
Address: 4004 Willow Drive, Guntersville, Alabama
Cell phone: 573-555-0015
Personal Note – Hesitates...has a stutter problem.
Family: Dysfunctional
Friend: None
Uncle: John Dono, Aunt: Gertrude Dono, Cousins: Ruth and Nathaniel
Uncles Jam Session Friends: Guy Billings, Billy Joe Rigby, Toney Schwartz.

Without further conversation, we shook hands, and Barry left. I stopped the recording of our conversation, took the documents that he had given us, made copies, and then placed the originals, along with the tape, into his file.

Family should stick together, and having none myself, I felt the pang of sorrow in their relationship with Barry more than most.

Lori took the copies, placed them on our board, and carefully studied them. She had a great memory for details, which I hoped would help us solve the case. The dates, the numbers, the picture, and a place to start... the family. She took the board into her office and I turned off the recorder since she was going to do some research on the computer.

Minutes later Lori found "Spurn's Guide to Mandolins" on line along with their product book. The particular one we were searching for was, according to them, worth $22,000.00 instead of $30,000.00. We discussed if we should tell him about that or not. I told her that I thought he probably already knew about the price and gave us the information to follow up on, knowing you would do that. I think either he wanted to impress us with an inflated figure, or he was waiting to see if we did our due diligence.

I could tell that she was letting what I said soak in. She stood on one foot, and used the top of her other foot to massage her ankle That was the habit that let me know she was attempting to analyze something. Finally she conceded I could be on the right tract, and agreed that it could have just been bait!

I really didn't mean it to seem like bait, but rather, a check on our investigative ability.

We needed a plan… you can't just get in the car and drive to his relatives and start interrogating them. We had to get into the household, and get some information, without any suspicion. Someone in the group knew something about those instruments, and I wanted to find out who that was and what they knew. I asked Lori how soon she could memorize the important facts and figures from the information we found, and from what Barry had told us.

She looked out of her office doorway and asked me why I asked about her ability to memorize those details from the book and our board details by the next day. I told her that I had an idea, but first, she needed to be certain of those facts and suggested that she do whatever she felt necessary to memorize that information.

I felt a little guilty, slipping out on her at a time like this, but the furniture was supposed was to be delivered to the new place and I had to be there because there was still my other things that had to be moved from the old apartment.

CHAPTER 9

I didn't miss the old apartment with the stairs worn down to the nub, and so misaligned, you almost had to be a gymnast to get up and down them. I didn't have to put up with them any longer. I finally had a place to call my own and one that Lori approved of. I knew it was much better than that other place I almost rented.

     I drove to the greasy spoon to have breakfast. Joe, the owner and cook, was standing behind the kitchen's long serving-window, half-yawning and half-awake and asked what he could get for me, so early that morning. I looked at his unshaven face, and the eyes that were still half-asleep, and asked for some plain buttered toast and coffee. He told me that didn't sound like much and asked if I was havin' a bad day.

     I've known Joe a long time, having had my office next door for over three years, and eating in the place frequently before moving my office there.. I answered it was a great day but I was moving into a new apartment over by old Highway 227 going up the mountain. Joe looked up from the grill, and told me that might be good for me, but not good for him. He said he had grown used to havin' me in there giving him a hard time and asked what he was going to do now.

His joking nature was intact, and whether I liked it or

not, I knew I would miss him. He had a way about him that made you like him, even if he didn't shave all the time, and was a bit unkempt. The food wasn't that great, but he made you believe that you were his best customer and his food was the best in town.

I told him he shouldn't sweat it, because I'd still come in from time to time…if for no other reason than just to be insulted. Joe smiled and went behind the serving window to prepare my order. He came back around the corner with a cup of coffee strong enough to force a bull to its knees. I blew into the cup, to cool it as he came back with a slice of buttered toast, slightly burned, two easy-over eggs, and the usual little packet of grape jelly. I gave him a 'thumbs up' as he turned around to return to the kitchen, acknowledging that he had once again outdone himself. I finished my toast and eggs, and slowly drank the hot coffee. It was not only very hot, but stronger than usual…I guess he thought I needed a kick-start for the day!

Joe's place behind me, I turned the key in the ignition and my Olds roared to life in protest with a backfire, and a burst of blue smoke. This was a new adventure, for old lizzy and me, and I was sure that it was going to be a good one. In minutes we were at the old apartment. The steps seemed much longer and steeper now. It's strange how you can live someplace and never notice anything unpleasant. You find a new Shangri-La, and the old place looks like a dump!

I carried the remaining boxes from the apartment to the car. I pushed, shoved, and crammed them into every cranny, excluding the driver's seat. I had boxes stacked to the ceiling and in the trunk, A bungee cord held the deck-lid closed as I drove to 1020 Franklin Place, my first ground floor apartment!

Flowers in the yard, a park just down the block to walk in, or to sit on one of the benches and rest. No high-rise places next door. There they are in the distance, but not on top of me, like in the old place.

The boxes had been doing a kind of juggling act all the way from the old place. I don't know how they managed to stay intact, with all the bumps, stoplights, jerks, and fast stops in traffic. I pulled on the end of the bungee cord and the hook came loose from the eye of the trunk latch. It opened wider than I had anticipated, and one box started to tumble. I grabbed it before it hit the pavement. Unfortunately, the two behind it did fall, but I saved one from the punishing drop to the street. So much for my reflexes!

I had a two-wheeler, on loan from the owner. I loaded four more boxes onto the two-wheeler, then for the next half hour, I unloaded more and placed their contents strategically throughout the apartment. Finally that one box I had been waiting for…the last one!

What a mess, even though a refreshing one.

Finally I had everything unpacked and put away,

then I discovered a box that I didn't remember. I took the box cutter from my pocket and carefully pushed the lever on the top moving the blade forward. As I pulled the sharp instrument through the taped ends of the box, I asked myself why I didn't remember this one. I pulled back the cardboard flaps and peered carefully into the box. The item was thin, fairly long, and well wrapped.

I didn't remember filling a box like this and sealing it so well. Was it possible that someone else left it here by mistake, and it wasn't mine? Should I have opened it? Did I want to know what was in the wrapping? How ridiculous! A grown man worried about what was in a box. If it wasn't mine I would have given it to the landlord and told him what happened.

I reached to remove the wrappings, but the more I thought about what might be in the box, the worse my fears became. I pulled the paper loose and discovered it was a Miami Herald newspaper.

I have never had a Miami Herald Newspaper...this can't be mine!

When the wrapping came loose, I looked to see was inside and when I saw it, I couldn't believe my eyes!

CHAPTER 10

The first thing in any investigation was to have a plan. I had one, and a lot of thought went into it. It was obvious, that Barry was estranged from the family, probably due to their totally different cultures. It was their continuous desire for money that was bothering me. It was necessary that I meet them in some way, other than with my true identity. They certainly would not give me any information if they knew I was working for Barry. I left my new apartment and arrived at the office at almost at the same time Lori did. I reminded her that we needed a plan, and told her that I had one. She called me Sherlock Holmes and made a sarcastic remark about my planning. I could see her wry sense of humor was in full swing that morning, so I asked her if she had memorized the information. She answered curtly, that of course she did, and that she had spent the whole night memorizing details... then, wanting a compliment, asked if that wasn't why I hired her, for her mind. I agreed with her but...

The fact that she was gorgeous, young, and bright might have had something to do her being hired in the first place; even we older guys like to have lovely things around us... it keeps us believing we are still young! I frequently have to remind myself that she is eight years younger than I am.

She was anxious to hear what I had come up with, and asked me to tell her what I had on my mind so I explained that she was about to become an instrument company employee of a stringed-instrument dealer with a special eye toward banjos. Especially about a certain one made in either the 40's or 50's. Lori eyed me suspiciously and asked where I was going with that.

I told her that since we had the full description of the mandolin, and a pretty good one for the banjo, we could use that knowledge in our investigation of the relatives, as well as the friends of Barry, and his Uncle John. Almost immediately she started that rubbing the top of her right ankle with her left foot. Then she asked me exactly what my plan was.

She wouldn't believe that I had an answer, but I did!

I explained that I was going to visit the guys John played with because, according to Barry, the aunt was a snob, while the uncle was a 'down to earth, good guy and they may have strong opinions about the family. I explained further that these men were probably his outlet from snobville, and I doubted that they would pull any punches.

That piqued her curiosity and she asked what she would be doing, while I was being one of the boys.

I told her that while I was doing my things, that she was going to be looking to purchase, for her company located somewhere in Tennessee, a particular instrument, the banjo.

She asked me why the banjo, instead of the mandolin. I answered that everyone would remember the banjo, since it was so different, but there were a lot of mandolins out there that pretty much look alike, consequently, they would not be easy to spot. That would make it possible for you to say that some of your friends remembered seeing John playing it, and it has taken time to track it down. By accident, you met some musician at one of your professional meetings that thought the Dono family might know where it was.

She looked at me questioningly and told me that she didn't have any professional groups, so maybe she should come up with her own ideas for that part of the plan. Then she had a brainstorm, she would tell them that her uncle was visiting and he went to a place where they jammed. It was there, that he saw this unusual banjo.

I could see my idea was working and that she filled in the blind spot with something that she could live with.

Lori looking down at the floor, questioned what if they put her on the spot and immediately had the instrument for her. That really bothered her so I stopped her fear by letting her know I had thought it out pretty well, with the pros and cons. I reassured her that they wouldn't do that because they were so greedy that even if they did know where it was, they would try to play some kind of game with her, and when that happened she would know they had it, or they would at least know where it was.

I always hate it when she does that ankle business, it makes me wonder what's going on in that pretty little head of hers.

She looked at me, moving that foot around to massage her ankle, and asked what I would be doing while she was engaging the enemy. I told her that I would be trying to get information out of the uncle's cronies. I still played the guitar a little then, when I had the time, and while I was not very good, it might have gotten them to talk to me... that was, assuming that they had their instruments when I found them... and they would accept me.

Lori continued that ankle massage. I knew she was analyzing the plan, and trying to figure out the outcome, but I knew the plan would work, as long as I got the information out of them while she got answers from the relatives, we could get a firm lead on where to find the instruments.

She stopped massaging her ankle, and moved toward the white-board. She turned to face me and said she could do it because she had learned enough about the instruments that she could talk with the best of them. She agreed to give it try. I left the office and drove to my place to get my guitar. Lori went to change her appearance. I found the relic in my closet, in its carrying case. It was so out of tune that all of the cats in the neighborhood started to meow in concert with the dogs howling. Fortunately, I had an iPad that had a tuner app. I tapped on it and a tuner appeared on the screen. Below it was a picture of several stringed instruments so I selected [guitar] and as easy as pie, the notes came as I asked for them. The instrument was tuned in short order. Having been a long time since I played the thing, I was surprised how easily I picked up where I had left off, so long ago.

Can I play well enough to get in with the group? Who knows?

I went back to the office and was totally surprised to see an older looking lady with glasses, sitting at Lori's desk. I asked if I could help her. She just smiled, then after a few moments of my staring at her, she asked if I thought she could pass for that musical person I dreamed up.

It was Lori! If she hadn't told me, I would never have believed the transformation she had made. She had streaked her hair with something that made it look blondish grey, recreated her makeup completely, and changed into clothing that would be more for a woman in her late forties than in her twenties. Even her shoes were different, they were the 'almost' flat kind with a very small heel. She was now a couple inches shorter. Wow, what a change!

She asked me how she looked, perhaps like a musically inclined businesswoman, or maybe, a choir director.

She had outdone herself. What a change! I barely recognized her at all.

It was time to play our parts, me a lonesome guitar player, and her, the dignified musical instrument dealer.

May the good Lord help us both!

It was easy enough for me to fill the bill. My old car fit right in with the type of person I was supposed to be. The addresses of Guy was in my billfold, and I was on my way. His place wasn't too far from the office, so I drove there in record time. The house, probably built back in the forties, had that cookie cutter look that made it comfortable and attractive. A thin fellow about five foot four opened the door and asked if he could help me. I asked if he was Mr. Billings, and he indicated that he was. Then he asked me who I was. Almost forgetting my undercover name, I quickly recouped my senses and told him I was Bud Anderson. I told them some country buddies of mine told me about the group and I was wondering if I could sit in for a jam session with them. He asked me who told me about them. Before I could answer, they told me they could sure use another member in their jam session group.

The living room was not a large one. The walls were decorated like an old entertainer might do. An old violin on one wall, pictures of some old time musicians, and a handful of newer entertainers, on another wall. The windows were narrow and high. The old lace curtains behind them were fresh and clean. It was clean and neat with that [old house] feeling and smell to it. I noticed that the carpet was not installed, but rather, laid from wall to wall so it could be removed easily for cleaning. There was a wooden rocking chair in one corner next to a reading table with some books arranged neatly on a shelf below the tabletop. There was an old overstuffed couch under the windows, where two gentlemen were sitting.

I told him, that a week or so ago, I met a young fella that played music in one of the small bars around town and that the fellow and I got to talking about music when he mentioned that his uncle used to play with you fellows. He thought that if I asked, I might be able to sit in with you, so he gave me your name and address.

Billings immediately responded that he guessed I had been 'talkin' to young Barry,' then immediately invited me to come in. He started to introduce me to the other two, but forgot my name. Then he remembered it was Bud, so he finished the introductions to Billy Joe Rigby and Tony Schwartz. Billy Joe stood, shook my hand, and told me they were glad to welcome me, and went on to say that they had been playin' there at Guy's place since their old friend, John, went to meet his maker. Tony followed suit saying about the same thing, then asked what my name was again

I told them how nice it was to meet them and told them that I didn't play very well, but did enjoy being with folks that could. I was told that they not only could, but did. I soon realized that they wanted to be treated like country folks, so I played along with them. They were wonderful and considerate old fellows, and they made you feel like you were an old friend, right from the beginning.

Both Guy and Tony asked, at the same time, what I played. I knew they hoped for a mandolin player, but I did well to [halfway] play the guitar. I told them someday I hoped to play the mandolin, and I left an opening there for some comment about old John and his instruments, hoping that one of them might tell me something.

Guy told me that John played the mandolin, and also an old banjo he found somewhere on a visit to South Carolina back in the 80's. Both of those instruments were beautiful, and he loved them. They indicated it was too bad I didn't play one of those instruments, then he told me that Billy Joe played the mandolin a bit. Billy Joe looked at Guy, with an understanding glance, then he answered that he didn't, it was Tony. I could see that Guy was a bit embarrassed, but Billy Joe had a quick comeback saying it didn't make any difference since he forgot his own name sometimes.

Leaving them with the thought that I would love to learn the mandolin, I suggested that if they knew where I could find one like old John had, I would consider some lessons. They still didn't take the bait, instead they asked me if I brought along my guitar, and for a mini-second, I forgot that I was Bud Anderson; I recovered from my brain fade a second time, and told them that it was in the car, and asked them if I should get it. They laughed and told me that if I didn't have my toy I couldn't play. All three of them got up and went into another room, then returned with their instruments. Guy had his guitar, Billy Joe, another beautiful banjo, and Tony his violin.

Excusing myself, I left to get my guitar. I kept my fingers crossed that I could keep up with these old musicians. I figured that I would know soon enough.

While I was investigating the old fellows, Lori decided that her little 'beetle' wasn't the type of car a businesswoman, from Tennessee, would drive, so she rented a smart looking SUV, small enough for her to navigate easily, and classy enough to make her appear prosperous. She realized that it was nice to have an expense account, of sorts. She drove to the address Barry had given her, double-checked it, and drove up the drive, rather than park on the street.

As she got out of the car she discovered her skirt had moved up considerably. She pushed it back in place, put on her glasses, and walked to the front door. When she rang the bell she noticed the curtain move on the front window. Those folks apparently liked to see who was at the door before opening it. An attractive young lady, dressed to the nines, opened the front door and asked Lori what she wanted.

Lori told her that she was looking for the Dono Family, and asked if she was at the right address, then leaned back, pretending to look at the house numbers beside the door.

The young lady confirmed it was the Dono residence, and again asked what Lori wanted. Lori gave her the undercover name of Judy Chillicothe and told her that she represented the Golden String Gallery of Cincinnati, then told her the matter was quite confidential and asked if she could come in.

Warily, she let Lori in and motioned toward a chair close to the door, suggesting that Lori sit there while she convened the family. The room was octagonal in shape. It had four doors, all facing from the back of the room to the front. There were two beautiful sitting areas, each in front of two outcropped windows. The drapes on the two large windows, one on each side of the front door, were exquisitely designed and made of a thick material with a silky texture. The floor was walnut hardwood, highly polished and with matching woodwork.

Rather than leave Lori alone, she knocked on two of the doors and asked the occupant of each to come into the living room. From behind the first door, a gruff woman's voice asked what the young lady wanted and informed her that she was busy.

She told her that the person had a personal message for all of them. The other woman ordered the young lady to tell her, again, that she was too busy!

Lori stood and stared across the room at whom she assumed could be Ruth, and this time insisted that the family be together, as she had something very important for them all to hear. Ruth was upset at being spoken to in that manner. She raised her arm and extended her finger toward the door and that was offensive to Lori.

The young lady screamed at her saying that she was unaccustomed to being ordered about, and demanded to know what the visit was about!

Lori was not easily dissuaded from her goal, and finding the Donos extremely rude, created a definite challenge for her. She overlooked the young woman's pointing her toward the door to dismiss her as one would a servant, and countered that she would not answer the reason for her visit until the three of them were present. Then, with a noticeably indignant twang to her voice, she added, if it wouldn't put them out too much! No doubt she hoped to rile the group enough to face her.

Ruth turned her back to Lori and told her that the family was not used to being summoned! Lori replied sarcastically, "Excuse me! I did not mean to summon anyone." She told them her time was short and valuable, and she had traveled some distance to see them... all of them.

From another room a man's voice emanated asking, Ruth, who was out there. Then telling her that she knew they didn't receive anyone without an appointment.

Living in that place would be very discouraging. It was no wonder that [Uncle John] disappeared frequently to be with real people.

Finally, Aunt Gertrude, and spoiled Nephew

Nathaniel, came out of their private 'dens of iniquity' and into the reception area. There could not be three more disparaging people assembled in one place. Gertrude appeared in a ridiculous gown that befit its wearer. Her hair was unkempt, and she had on worn out slippers. Nephew Nathaniel wore a sweater that apparently came from his college dorm, and appeared to not have been taken off since then. His trousers were without the normal press line on the leg fronts, and the rest of the trouser was not pressed. His entire attire looked as though it was just retrieved from a laundry basket. Only the young lady, now identified as Ruth, dressed like she belonged in that beautiful home. Neither her manners nor her disposition matched her clothing, unfortunately!

Gertrude, once again asked what she wanted as they were very busy people and didn't have time to waste on callers.

Lori told them that she didn't come there to upset them, but rather to speak to them about a possession Gertrude's deceased husband was known to possess. As we had previously decided, she spun the tale about her representing a large instrument company in the East, and she would like them to consider her company's purchase of that special instrument.

Nathaniel lived up to his reputation as a smart-ass individual and asked if Lori thought they looked like [low life] musicians. Not to be intimidated by this trio of creatures from the black lagoon, she looked into Gertrude's eyes, and boldly announced, that she was looking for a long necked banjo with an engraved

Indian headdress with ivory inlays on the back, and adorned with several small lights attached at precise intervals around the body.

The three of them, smelling a buck to be made, huddled in the center of the room like a group of witches at a kettle. Gertrude finally turned toward Lori and demanded that she tell them how she came upon the knowledge that they might know something about this instrument.

Lori told them that Gertrude's late husband's instrument was one that any real musician would recognize for what it was. Just seeing it caused it to be described by the person who saw it to his friend, her uncle. He, being a connoisseur of instruments said he only knew of one man that owned one like that, and that was John Dono in Alabama!

All three, almost with saliva dripping from their lips like nightmare creatures, asked in unison, what kind of offer she was considering.

She explained that that couldn't be divulged until she saw and examined the instrument since the company would not be interested if it was damaged.

Again, they stood in the center of the room with their backs to Lori, and talked in a whisper. After some time, Gertrude, turned to face Lori. She told her that they would have to go somewhere else to get the instrument, because they had it in safekeeping since poor John's death. They asked Lori if she had a phone number where she could be reached. Lori, suspecting that they really had no idea where the instrument was gave a card with the office's old landline phone number on it, but she asked if it would be alright to call them the next day, around 3:00 PM. Not wanting to lose out on a possible gain in their fortunes, They gave her their phone number and agreed.

Lori thanked them for their time and left. She got into the rental and drove around the block, parking behind a property fence a few doors from the Dono house. She felt that at least one, or more of them, would be coming out very soon, to go wherever the instrument was, or at least where they thought it might be.

Her hunch was right, they came out quibbling about which one sat where. Gertrude drove the black continental, her babbling daughter in the front beside her, and Nathaniel in the back. They headed toward downtown, with Lori, keeping a safe distance, following behind.

CHAPTER 11

I was glad they played by ear since if I had to sight-read music and play, it would have been my downfall.

The three old musicians seemed to like me. Once they heard me play, I was concerned I wouldn't make the cut. They were so anxious to fill that fourth spot that they would have accepted anyone. They asked, when we had finished, if I would be willing to add to the pot. I reached into my back pocket to get my wallet and they stopped me. They explained that once a month, they each put ten dollars into the pot. They used that to buy music, strings, picks, etc. They said that I could not put anything into the pot, that is, unless I planned to be a member of the group! I gave them ten bucks.

When I opened my car door to put the guitar and its case into the back seat, I turned and saw all three of them looking out of the front window, smiling and apparently happy with my invasion of their group. I felt guilty taking advantage of them, but it had to be done.

What if they caught onto her act? What if they have called the cops, or worse they could be holding her at their place trying to get information out of her?

It worried me that Lori wasn't at the office by the time I returned. My thoughts ran wild. I poured a cup of coffee and waited. It seemed like an eternity, since time goes by so slowly when you are waiting for someone.

The phone rang; I looked at it, anticipating the worst, and let it ring a couple more times. Dreading that my worries could be true, I picked it up and answered with the usual Deavereau office greeting of, Deavereau Detective Agency, this is Deavereau, how can I help you. There was a hesitation. I waited impatiently for someone to say something. The sweat beaded on my forehead, then finally a voice answered. Mr. Deavereau, this is... Barry, any news yet.

It was good to hear his voice; it stopped my worries about Lori, at least for that moment. I told him it was good to hear from him and that we had not found anything new yet but I was waiting to hear from Lori right then. Another hesitation, sometimes I wish Barry would just speak, instead of hesitating so much.
He told me that he knew it was early, and although he might be expecting too much too quickly, he thought he would call and check in.

I felt like agreeing with him, but it wasn't the thing to do so I told him that he had every right to call since we were working for him. I told him that we would keep him posted and that he would be the first to know if we found out anything. Again, the hesitation, then, he said, okay, he would wait to hear from us. He hung up the same way he answered, abruptly but only after a bit of silence. Another hour passed by, a second cup of coffee, a nervous walk around the office, another cup.

Where could she be?

CHAPTER 12

No different from other waiting rooms in a hospital, it was a little chilly, people waiting to hear about health, death, miracles, or whatever fate the patient they are waiting for, might receive.

There were only two other people remaining in the waiting room. Earlier, I watched one older man, with five of his family members, or perhaps, friends. It was a matter of "what will be, will be," as one of the family whispered. The older gentleman appeared to be less mentally stable than the rest. He constantly smiled and agreed with whatever was said, although he probably didn't understand a thing being discussed. They spoke, he nodded in agreement. Before they left the induction area, it was certain that the concern they all had, was about him.

Seated on a soft large chair was another visitor. She also was waiting for someone, but kept herself busy on her cell phone, using an ear companion, that so many people have; it appeared that it could be an attached appendage, rather than a portable device used for practical purposes.

As always, there was a coffee machine that dispenses mild, medium, or bold coffee. There was no tea, no hot chocolate, just coffee. Interesting that the doctors all tell you to stop drinking so much coffee, since it isn't good for you, yet fail to have another drink available.

The television set was on, and of course it was playing a station that no one was interested in. One could change the station, but no one wanted to take the chance, with the fear that the change could offend someone who really might be interested in whatever it was that was being broadcast.

There could have been no nicer waiting room. It was large, could probably have seated sixty-five people or more; God forbid that there should be that many people in that particular wing of the hospital at one time, needing that kind of care. How was Lori doing? I was concerned about her. The nurse should have called in by now! Could she be worse than I thought?

I was awakened from my thoughts by a voice asking to be excused, and then the voice asked if I was sleeping. Then how sorry to awaken me. I looked through dazed eyes, my mind dealing with the families in the waiting room, and answered the voice that I wasn't sleeping....discovering the voice was the nurse, I asked for news about Lori. She told me Lori was fine, a bit shaken up with a bruise here and there, and then elaborated on they were so glad that I had brought her here.

I told the nurse that she was tougher than she looked, and asked if I could see her. She answered I could, but only for a short time, because she needed to get more rest to fully recuperate, then she gave me the room number, 218.

I stood, still a bit dazed, then looking at the nurse I told her that we were lucky to have folks like her to look after us. I knew the family that was with the older gentleman were very thankful too. I turned and shuffled down the corridor toward Room 218.

Lori had her bed in the semi-sitting position drinking from one of those wonderful hospital cups with the straw sticking out of it. She greeted me with, hi partner, she guessed she wasn't too great at sleuthing, then ended with she did get caught. I told her, with the most sympathetic voice I could muster, that wasn't important, but what was important was that she was safe. She looked so pitiful, half-laying, and half-sitting on her bed.

She answered that she knew me better than that, and stated that I had about as much sympathy as a cat on a hot tin roof with a hot cup of milk to drink. I kidded her with, I was human and knew she would prefer to believe bad things about me. We both laughed.

On a more serious note, I told her that according to the nurse, she didn't know how she got to the hospital, and I asked if she did or not. She answered that all she could remember was somehow she escaped from those people, by running into the woods. She cupped her hand around the side of her mouth, to muffle what she was going to say, then she asked if there were any cops there.

I turned to look out of the door, and then through the small observation window. There was no one to be seen, except the occasional nurse making her rounds. I returned my gaze back to Lori and told her that the cops have all gone home, they don't work 24-7 you know! Then I asked her why she was concerned. She told me she didn't know why. For some reason or other she felt she was being watched. I told her she had nothing to worry about, she was safe, and no one was around but me.

It was as though a cool breeze entered the room, and the air from it seemed to lighten the load. I could tell Lori was beginning to relax now, and she needed her rest. She fell asleep, so I left her with her thoughts.

She didn't need to know that she called me on the cell phone and I found her in the woods and she fainted in my arms.

Morning came, too early as usual. The alarm clock lived up to its name and the noise shocked me to awareness at 6:30 AM. I stretched, mumbled a few unnecessary words, and rolled over, dropping my head toward the floor. The night was all too short, I didn't sleep well, worrying about Lori, and knowing that wild family I sent her to see, was the cause of her problem.

The cold floor felt good on my feet, even if it did shock the rest of my system. I got up and did the usual. Well, almost anyhow. I don't usually cut my chin with a razor when I shave, but that morning…well anything could have happened. I spilled a glass of water that I used to rinse my mouth with all over the vanity. It dribbled onto the floor at my feet. I leaned over to mop up the water with my towel and hit my head on the door to the vanity cabinet…it hurt!

It wasn't long before I was in the car and heading back to the hospital. I was hoping that Lori would be interested in a couple of eggs over easy, a cup of good coffee and maybe a pancake or two, thrown in for good measure, assuming they were going to release her.

I walked down the corridor to Room 218 to find her fully dressed and ready to go. She was arguing with the nurse's aide about the necessity of having to be wheeled out in a wheel chair. She told the nurse that she didn't need that thing and asked her if she thought that she looked like an invalid. The poor nurse, only doing her duty, answered it was hospital policy. She had to wheel her out. The young nurse's aide looked browbeaten and ready to cry. I took matters into my own hands by suggesting to Lori, that I carry her out, rather have the young lady wheel her out. I thought that mental picture would make her more reasonable. Lori very loudly asked me what I thought I was doing. Then she informed me that of course she didn't want me to carry her out!

The other nurses in the hallway were giggling ...

discreetly. They knew what I was doing, even if neither the young lady behind the wheel chair, nor Lori, didn't.

After getting her into the car, she started to settle down, and said she supposed that I had all kinds of advice for her. I just looked at her, smiled, and asked her if she would like a decent breakfast. She looked at me like I had just saved her life and told me yes, that was the best idea I had had for days, so let's do it!

I was shocked at such an immediate response, but pleased at the same time. I revved up the engine and probably broke some speed laws, but I wanted to get to the old greasy spoon before she changed her mind.

We both received a cup of coffee while waiting for our order. She looked a lot more relaxed, so I thought I might ask her what happened the day before. She took a sip of the hot coffee, laid her cup down, and proceeded to explain what she could remember.

She said, she had gone to the Dono home, and played her part, as we had discussed. It didn't go very well and she felt that the Dono family would either call someone, or leave to find someone regarding the banjo she had asked them about, so she moved the car far enough away that they couldn't see her, and waited. It was just a few minutes before their car backed out of the drive and into the street. She let them get a block or so ahead of her before she pulled out to follow them. Sure enough, they drove straight to a house on the corner that had been transformed into a kind of antique shop. They got out and went in the side door. She followed, just far enough behind the trio that she shouldn't be discovered. An unshaven and gray haired figure emerged from the shadows of the poorly lit room. Looking as if he had been interrupted from some devious deed, he opened the door and asked them what they wanted.

Lori said she circled the block and parked on a side street, out of view of the house. She got out of the driver's side, leaving her purse in the car, but holding onto her keys. It wasn't her original plan to get too close to her quarry, but there was no choice if she was to get the information she wanted. She snuck quietly around the side of the house where a small window was slightly cracked open. There she heard the back and forth bickering. Gertrude, with her authoritarian voice, called him an old fool, and to stand aside and let them in or he'd wish he hadn't even opened the door! She browbeat the figure and pushed him aside and stepped into the building.

He, being taken by surprise with her action, composed himself and told her that he saw that she had the same manners she always had, and continued to tell her that she may have treated her husband like an old dog, but she'd best not try to treat him that way! Gertrude had apparently met her match with the old shop owner's equally abusive aggression.

Nathaniel and Ruth followed behind, and closed the door. They stood behind Gertrude, as if acting as a back-up force to be reckoned with. Their expressions, were frozen in sneers that appeared to be chiseled on their disgusting faces.

*If witches existed in Guntersville,
these two women and their warlock relative would
surely be members of the cult!*

Gertrude, in her aggravating voice, informed the gray haired man, that they had sold him a banjo a month or so ago, and they wanted it back. Then she demanded to know where it was. The two cowards behind Gertrude chanted in unison, asking where it was.

The old man they were addressing put his hands on his hips, straightened up to his full height, and told them it was none of their business. Gertrude sold it to him; he in turn sold it to someone else, and there was nothing more to do about it.

The trio getting more irritated by the minute, and almost synchronized to sound as one, spoke, saying they wanted it back. The man walked to the door and opened it and told them to get out! He told them he didn't have time for them because he was busy with more important things.

Deciding to change her approach, Gertrude offered him twice what he gave her. He saw that she wanted to deal with him and closed the door. He said he would not consider her offer as it would cost twice that much for him to re-purchase the instrument. He told them that if they could not do better than that, then he had no more time for them.

Still thinking he could be maneuvered to their

liking, Gertrude offered three hundred dollars. The old man scoffed, then told them it would take at least four times the original price, he gave them, for him to even consider their offer. She shouted that four times was robbery! He smiled and told her that, coming from her that sounded funny, and he laughed.

Seeing there was no use to bicker, Gertrude agreed to pay the money, but still insisting it was robbery, she asked how soon he could get it back.

Lori told me that hoping to learn more, she stepped onto the sidewalk leading to the door when suddenly, it opened and she was face to face with the trio. There was no time to turn around; there was no place to hide. Completely caught off guard, she faced the three of them and was immediately questioned by Gertrude as to her presence there. Summoning up courage, she answered that she saw this shop with the sign saying that they had antiques and decided to see what they had. Before she could say any more, Gertrude interrupted, accusing her of following them.

In an attempt to defend herself, she asked, why would she want to follow them? All she wanted to do was visit the quaint looking shop. That was when Ruth asked her if that was the case, where was her car. Having no answer, she tried to move past them, but Gertrude grabbed her by the arm.

She told me she searched for a plan of escape, but before she could come up with one, Nathaniel grabbed her other arm. His mother and he, muscled her to their car. Ruth opened the trunk and Gertrude and

Nathaniel started to shove her body into it, but Nathaniel lost his footing on the wet leaves. Trying to keep his balance, he let go of Lori for a moment. Lori kicked Gertrude, knocking her to the ground. While they were in disarray, Lori moved quickly, half crawling and half running into the dark wooded area next to the antique shop parking area.

I was so captivated that I gulped down my cup of coffee, while absorbing every word. Joe interrupted her when he brought our breakfast out, so rather than continue, she stopped talking and waited for him to leave. I pointed to my cup, signaling that I needed a refill. He acknowledged with a nod. Being hungry I chowed down like a hound with a rabbit. To my surprise, Lori ate faster than I did, which was unusual. She finished, took a drink of her coffee, and then continued with her memory of what had happened.

I asked if she got hurt and she shook her head back and forth indicating a "no" answer. She said that she thought that she would be safe hidden in the woods, and that's the last thing she remembered.

She drove there, but she didn't drive away. Could her car still be on the street? I know that cars left on the street in Guntersville, after nine or so in the evening, are generally towed away to the impound lot. I don't know why I didn't think about that last night. I guess I was just too concerned about getting her to the hospital that nothing else entered my mind.

After we finished our breakfast, we decided that we should go see if her if car was still where she left it, and I asked her if she remembered where her purse was. She looked at me in complete surprise and answered that she didn't remember...but thought she left it in the car. We jumped into my car and headed toward the corner antique store. It was just a few blocks from the greasy spoon that we had just had breakfast in.

We came to the old house with the porch swing, and thankfully, Lori's rental was still where she had parked it, just down the street. Both of us echoed a sigh of relief as I pulled up close to her car. Lori slipped out and walked to the driver's door. It was still unlocked and, as we suspected, in her hurry to continue her surveillance, she left her purse in the car, but where was the ignition key?

Lori said it was a remote thingy so she didn't have to have the key in the ignition switch. She only had to have it with her. If she left it in her purse, the car would have honked at her. She nervously explained to me that that was what the new cars did, they warned you if you have left your key inside and walked away. She said that it didn't honk yesterday, or she would have heard it, then she questioned where she could have left it. She thought, maybe the hospital?

I gave her question a few seconds of thought, then told her that I knew she didn't want to hear it, but if she had it at the hospital, the nurse would have given it to her. Then I asked her if it was possible that it could have fallen into the trunk of the Dono's car during the struggle. She considered that could have happened; if she had the key in her hand, not considering she might be abducted, she could well have lost it in the struggle. Then she asked me how we were going to get it back.

Realizing that Lori was beside herself with worry, I suggested she might call the car agency and tell them that she lost it. She answered with a "you bet!" Then she continued by asking me if I knew that little trinket cost $250.00. I was shocked and asked her if she was kidding me. Lori, being already mad, exploded, and almost shouting, she told me that she wasn't kidding and started in on me again about my old, beat up Olds, with a key from the past century. I dropped my head like a whipped dog that did something unnecessary, and I told her that I was sorry and didn't think about that. She immediately informed me that was the problem, I didn't think!

I realized that Lori didn't want to accept the responsibility, and that arguing wasn't going to get the key back. I had to come up some way of getting that key back. I looked into Lori's eyes, bloodshot as they were after her ordeal, and told her I had an idea that I thought would work, even if it sounded a little quirky.

Lori, rubbed her ankle, with the heel of her shoe, like she always did when trying to analyze something. I outlined my idea, that since the Dono family didn't know me, I could go to their car, and open the trunk to check for the key. I would close the trunk, then open the side door, and then, before they could get out of their house, I could have the key.

Lori looked befuddled and asked what if they were to see me and shoot me or something? I answered that I had that covered too. If they came out, I would tell them I would like to test drive it, and ask them if they were sure of the price that they put in the ad.

Lori looked at me quizzically, and asked me why they would they believe that nonsense. I explained that they were going to scream they didn't run any ad in the paper, and they were would threaten to call the cops. I would look unconcerned, apologize that I must have had the wrong address, and then ask them if they knew of a neighbor with a car, like theirs, that might be for sale. I was sure they would buy my story, so I asked her if she agreed. Lori had no option at that point. She agreed the idea was workable but, her concern was this trio of horrible people were very suspicious, very unconventional, and very, very dangerous. She thought I might be taking my life into my own hands, knowing what she did, about that degenerate family. My plan was begrudgingly agreed upon so now it was my turn to meet the wonderful Dono family.

Lori filled me in on the location of the house, what the family was like, and what kind of reaction I should expect. (I thought that she was describing a nightmare family that Hollywood directors might dream up) I told her that I understood, and told her not to worry. I would be safe.

I pulled up in front of the place and wondered why people like the Donos deserved this beautiful home, when they are so greedy and disgusting.

Oh well, such is life.

Their car was parked in the drive. Luckily for me, the window drapes in the house were pulled over the living room window and I hoped that I wouldn't have to pull the ruse that I had described to Lori. They drove a big black Lincoln, one that I couldn't afford. I couldn't remember how to open the trunk, then, remembering something that I saw on TV, I moved my foot back and forth under the rear of the car. Nothing happened! I felt under the little ledge over the top of the license plate. There was a small rubber like raise, I pushed on it. The trunk lid opened. Gleaming in the afternoon sunlight like a beacon, the key fob stuck out like a sore thumb against the black fabric of the trunk. I picked it up and stuck it into my pocket. I walked around to the side door and started to open it, when the door to the house opened.

An older woman shouted at me asking, what the hell I thought I was doing. She told me to stop standing there smiling and then turned to the young man standing slightly behind her, and shouted for him to call the police. The young man started to open the front door, so I started my spiel about wanting to buy the car. She answered me telling me that I must be an idiot! Did I think they would put an ad in the paper? They didn't like company or people, and they certainly wouldn't take out an ad that would attract them.

I told her that I was very sorry and suggested that since she was not Mrs. Riley, would she happen to know of a Mrs. Riley that lived close by, and with this exact car for sale. She screamed for me to get out of there and asked me what part of [we don't like people] didn't I understand. I rushed away, hiding the smirk I had on my face. The key was in my pocket and my scheme worked. and I, at long last, knew what the matriarch of the family looked like. It took me very little time to drive out of the neighborhood and back to Lori and the rental. As I handed her the key, she sighed a sigh of relief. We both were glad it was over.

Those Dono folks were something to be reckoned with. I laugh when I think about when that trunk and the other door opened up when I didn't have a key....maybe the key fob, left in the drink holder of their car, had something to do with it?

CHAPTER 13

I was surprised to see Barry so early. It was barely eight o'clock in the morning. As he entered the office, he had an obvious grin on his face. He told me he had come because Aunt Gertrude called him to say they were being harassed. I looked at him with a surprised look. I get that from time to time, when I think someone is trying to pull the wool over my eyes, so I asked him if he was kidding me.

He said no, she told him that someone was trying to steal their car and she wondered if he had something to do with it. Now, he just wanted to say thanks to us for harassing her. Even though she already knew the answer, Lori asked why he felt the need to say thanks.

Barry sat down in the side chair by her desk, removed his glasses, and laid them on her desk. He switched his gaze from Lori to me and told us that he could not be more pleased. Those scoundrel relatives had made his life, as well as his dear uncle's life, a hell on earth. To the best of his memory he had never heard a kind word from any of them. They continuously degraded his uncle saying he was a bad musician, a horrible financial person, and a non-caring old putt. After stopping for a few seconds, he continued, saying that he was sure that it was me looking at the car, and added, "Wasn't it?"

I told him about the incident with Lori, and what had happened. He nodded, understanding the situation, but smiling as he imagined his aunt on the porch shouting obscenities.

He had come to the office to gloat over our victory, and also to vent his feelings about the family. He iterated how his uncle was the one that made the money, and the rest of the family spent it, that if it had not been for him, there'd be no fancy home, no Lincoln car, and certainly no money. He gave a lot to charity; he founded several foundations for various causes and above all, he was a kind and forgiving man. Barry wondered how his aunt and their kids could treat him like they did and told us that his uncle always treated him like a son.

I looked at Barry with sympathy for his plight. We both had heard most of it before, but here was a guy that tried to pattern his life after his uncle, while the rest of the family returned his graciousness with hatred and animosity. Lori, as usual, remained business oriented and told Barry we were going to do all we could to retrieve those things that were supposed to be his, then she requested permission to ask him a question. He said he would answer anything she asked.

Lori told him that we had met them and found they were pretty much as he had described. Her question was, why would they take that beautiful instrument to an old antique store, instead of, a music store that handles fine instruments? Barry looked up at her like a sheep waiting to be sheared and told her that he had no idea, unless it was the shop in Guntersville owned by an old man, a Mr. Appleby.

We both asked in unison, who is Mr. Appleby?

Barry stood, his face turned red with an irritation that I had not seen before. He told us that Mr. Appleby used to be in business with his uncle. Uncle John put up the money, and Appleby took on the chore of running the business. Prior to that time, Ben had approached his uncle, on several occasions, about helping him monetarily. It appeared that his uncle was cheated out of the money that he had invested, and Ben then became friends with, (as much as one could become friends with) his aunt.

It seemed clear that the business venture may have stood in the way of his uncle's friendship with Appleby. I was beginning to understand the connection between his aunt and the shopkeeper. I asked if his Aunt Gertrude and this Mr. Appleby had a personal relationship. Barry looked embarrassed at the thought, but answered yes, he thought I was probably right, then he said it had to be a personal relationship... made in hell! His comment made me smile since it was out of context for Barry.

We advised him that we had several people under surveillance and that I had been in contact with the old group his uncle played with, while Lori was in close contact with his Aunt Gertrude, and the Cousins Ruth and Nathaniel. Through our surveillance, we discovered that his Aunt had pawned the banjo with

Mr. Appleby, and that they went to retrieve it but were told that he sold it. They gave him notice to get it back, but Mr. Appleby was not being cooperative in that endeavor. There appeared to be bad blood between his aunt and Appleby, and we planned to use that in our favor. Until we locate that purchaser, we weren't letting anything slip by us.

Barry agreed that Lori and I had covered a lot of ground since our first meeting and he asked how close we might be in the recovery of the instruments. I didn't want Barry to be over confident so I told him that time would tell, and that we had just scratched the surface, and there was still lot of ground to cover! He stood and put his hand out to be shaken. He looked at one of us, and then at the other, and told us that he was confident we would find the instruments. Then he left.

I asked Lori if she needed a little more rest and she replied that she didn't, and although she overslept that morning, it wasn't going to happen again!

The coffee was on, our client, had left, and we needed to make some new plans for retrieval of the banjo and the mandolin. I didn't manage a cup of coffee before Barry showed up. I was sure that Lori would complain about my coffee, but I really didn't care, I poured her a cup anyhow. I thought we might figure out where the banjo had been in the last week or so.

After taking a sip of my coffee, she made an

awful face, set her cup on my desk, and told me what awful stuff it was, asking why couldn't I at least get good coffee, so she could drink the stuff? I countered her attack on my coffee, telling her if she didn't like it…too bad! It's all we had, so if she didn't like it, pour it down the drain and drink some water!"

She laughed, assuming that I was kidding, but agreed she deserved a verbal dressing down! That being said, she sat her cup down and removed our whiteboard from the closet, thinking that we needed to work with it before we got too boggled down with unimportant things. She asked where we should start.

That old white board, on its wiggly easel, helped a lot. I didn't know if my memory wasn't as good as it used to be, or if Lori, who is so organized, created a new tool for our business. I do know, that having the information on the board was an asset for us both.

I looked at my watch and agreed with her. Following her lead, we put our heads together, and attempted to digest our notes. She erased the unimportant things on the board, and started writing down the personal information for Barry Dono, and the names of the Dono family, before I got my third cup of coffee. I suggested, considering the type of people we were dealing with, we might describe their personality as well. It was my thinking that remembering certain quirks could come in handy later.

Her reply wasn't what I expected! She told me she didn't think that was a bit funny and that she was trying to do a job and I was supposed to be helping her, not making jokes! I informed her I wasn't joking, that we needed to have that kind of information about each of them. I asked if she didn't think that was good detective work, to know what we could use, if we needed to, to cause deception between the family members. Lori started to massage the top of her right foot with her left one, as she thought about what I said.

She apologized to me, saying that she was so into the case because of the treatment she got from the Dono family, she got disgusted every time she thought about them. She agreed that I was right, but she wouldn't forget their traits, and she added that since I wasn't there, they weren't indelibly written in my mind, like they were in hers. I smiled and took another sip of my coffee. She knew that I was pleased with her apology.

She headed the next part, "Facts"

1. Mandolin, collector's item. Expensive. No clues yet
2. Banjo, Also collector's item. Checked out antique shop and owner, Mr. Ben Appleby
3. Dono Family, apparently sold banjo to Appleby
4. Lori's undercover name – Judy Chillicothe
5. Lori's undercover company - Golden String Gallery of Cincinnati
6. Bill's undercover name – Bud Anderson

7. Uncle John's group- Guy Billings, Billy Joe Rigby and Tony Schwartz

We didn't have a lot to go on, but we felt that someone in this group would lead us to the banjo. We agreed that Mr. Appleby was right in the middle of it all, and decided that he should be our next stop. We went under-cover as Bud Anderson and Judy Chillicothe.

Lori, thinking ahead, asked if I thought we could con Appleby, then before I could answer, she was out the door telling me to hurry up, she wanted to get going. She smiled, just to let me know she was anxious, not irritated.

Eager to get on with the case, I pulled the door to the office shut and we left.

As we climbed into my car she started asking when I was going to get the [old thing] either fixed or traded. In response to her belittling, it shook, and smoke poured from the exhaust. I told her I had a love affair with my old Olds, and couldn't think about trading her in. Lori cocked her head and answered me with a laugh, telling me I had to love something, but questioned why this old wreck…seemed to her that I needed a better car to make a good impression on our clients. I came up with a ridiculous retort telling her that in the first place, most of the people never see my car, and secondly, if they thought I could afford a newer car, they would complain about our fees. I asked, along that same line of thought, why didn't she replace that little tiny bug...that beetle. She told me I was [full of it] because her 'Volks' was only a year old, not ancient like my Olds.

She was right, but what the heck, I've been "full of it" for so long I doubt I'll ever change; besides, I love that old car.

     We arrived at the clapboard house with the swing on the porch before we knew it. As a couple, we entered the store needing to get a [lay of the land] before deciding our next action. There was no need to arouse any suspicions.

     Mr. Appleby greeted us at the door and ask us to come in, take a look around and make ourselves at home.

It was unbelievable this cheerful greeting came from him, considering what we'd been told about him. I wondered what other surprises we were in for.

     He welcomed us and told us it was always nice to meet new folks. He hesitated momentarily, and then extended his hand for me to shake it, introducing himself as Ben, and asked what our names were. I shook his hand and introduced us as Bud Anderson and Judy Chillicothe. He said it was a lovely day and Lori smiled, answering that it certainly was.

We started to carefully peruse the place but he followed us. He asked if there was anything special we were looking for. Not wanting to be identified as folks looking for an instrument, Lori answered, casually, that we were just browsing, and told him that we had just rented an apartment and thought there might be something we might be interested in, in his shop.

Ben answered that he would just leave us alone and let us look around, and if we didn't find what we were looking for, please tell him, and he would see if he could find it for us. We nodded we would, then walked through the aisles of merchandise that he had to offer. We came upon some old instruments. I picked up an old guitar and strummed it a couple of times. Ben asked if I had an interest in guitars. I told him that I played occasionally but thought about learning the banjo or mandolin. I explained that I had met some guys that needed a mandolin player, but accepted me and my guitar instead.

Ben smiled one of those, 'guess what I got' smiles, and suggested I might like to see a couple of instruments he had recently purchased but had not had time to put on display yet. I didn't want to be pushy, so I said that it sounded intriguing. He disappeared into another room and came out holding a beautiful banjo. It looked like it had been very well taken care of, and he suggested I should try it out. I explained that all I knew about a banjo was that the fingering was supposed to be the same as a mandolin… and I wasn't even too sure about that.

He was overly pushy that I should try it out anyway. I attempted an excuse suggesting that he probably didn't notice I had a bad finger. I held it up, bending it slightly at the top knuckle joint. I told him that I fell a week or so before, and jammed it pretty good. I went on to explain that unfortunately, it was one of the main fingers I needed to play my guitar and hopefully, in another week or so, it would heal.

I hoped he would appreciate my situation… and accept it, but now what? I didn't know how to play the darn thing, and I didn't want to get on Ben's bad side. Even though this was not the banjo I was looking for, it was a beauty.

He told me he was sorry to hear that, and hoped that since I strummed the guitar I could play, then he asked if my finger was sore. I told him yes, it was sore and it appeared that he bought it!

Lori, in the meantime, had looked at several things in the shop. She would pick up this or that, study it a bit, but when she found something she was pondering, the left foot would come up, and she would rub the sole of her shoe on the top of her right ankle. It was a dead giveaway to me, that she was giving a lot of thought to purchasing something. Finally she found an old 78 rpm record of a violinist. She asked Ben what he would take for it. He responded with $10.00 and she answered with, "That was a bit high!" Mr. Appleby seemed a bit flustered, or perhaps just embarrassed to be asked about his pricing and asked. what she thought it was worth?" She told him that $3.00 was all it was worth. It wasn't a famous musician, it would take an outdated machine to play it, and it wasn't in a jacket.

Old Ben looked like a whipped pup when he raised his gaze to look at hers. He told her that he had a lot of upkeep here. Every item was one of a kind, or at least he tried to keep it that way and suggested that she may not know this violinist, but that didn't mean she is not as good as they come, and that he had personally heard her. Lori, recognizing his tactic, answered that he may have heard her, but she heard her neighbor singing in the shower every day. That didn't make him great, except maybe to his own ears. Three dollars is all she would pay for it.

Ben Appleby had met his match. He lowered the price to $3.00, in submission to Lori's steadfast opinion. She bought it. Getting the record, at her price, started her into the undercover mode. She said, I introduced her, but didn't tell him that she was interested in old instruments too. Now, with great enthusiasm, and probably hoping to recoup some of his loss, he suggested that she might like to see some of the old ones he had accumulated.

Lori told him that she was a representative of a

firm, in one of the Eastern United States, which buys certain instruments, and added that they were very particular in what they purchased. She continued telling him that they were searching for a special banjo that had a longer neck than usual, with a beautiful Indian Head Dress etched, and painted, on the back of it and along the neck. They were also looking for a special Gibson Mandolin from 1920. She asked if he happened to have anything like that in his back room.

Not wanting to lose a prospective buyer, he smiled at Lori, then answered carefully that he couldn't tell her if he had either of those or not. He did seem to recollect a banjo, like the one she described, but he may have sold it. He said he would have to check his records to be sure and asked if she would be interested, should he happen to locate it.

Lori, not wanting to appear over enthusiastic, gave him her card and told him that he could reach her on her cell phone. He told her he would get back to her as soon as he could.

I was impressed. Lori was more of an undercover detective than I thought she was. She pulled this off as smoothly as a piece of silk on a tabletop! I wondered what she would come up with next.

I walked to the front door, with her in heel. We said our goodbyes and left the antique store letting the plan Lori had set in place, start working. When we were clear of the place, I told her how well she played her role, and that I had never seen her do a better job. Then

I told her that I hoped she didn't overdo by telling him about the fake company.

I hoped that Ben wouldn't contact Gertrude with this slip-up telling Ben too much!

CHAPTER 14

By the time the trio regained their balance, Lori was gone. The three of them jumped into the car and turning on the lights scanned the area, but to no avail. Disoriented and upset, Gertrude, with her disgusting voice asked what had happened.

Nathaniel answered, with an accusing voice, that if his mother hadn't let go of her...Gertrude finished the sentence with, "If [I] hadn't let go of her?" You nincompoop, you let go of her first. His excuse was that he slipped on something wet and fell...and that was not his fault, then still accusing his mother, continued with, "You, on the other hand..."

Ruth, exasperated with them both, told them both that neither of them were to blame, things happen. The real problem was what were they going to do now, Miss Chillicothe certainly won't be making a social call.

Nathaniel, suggested that they had to think quickly because she was gone, wasn't going to come back, and realized that they had no idea where that damned banjo was. Gertrude asked when did Nathaniel ever think quickly and called him an imbecile. He asked her to please not speak to him in that manner, and in no uncertain terms announced that he didn't like it!

She copied him, sarcastically mimicking, "You don't like it?" And as she spoke she moved one hand from the steering wheel, and smashed Nathaniel alongside the head, then she asked if he liked that better! Nathaniel cowered in his seat, frightened by his mother's sadistic behavior.

Ruth, joining in the melee, suggested, with her screechy voice, that they should stop the nonsense because they had a real problem, as she tried to tell them before, the fact the woman who was supposed to give them money for that ratty old instrument, was now aware of their treachery, had escaped their hold, and will undoubtedly tell someone about what they did to her. She asked them both how far were they going to go with this charade.

Visibly shaken by what they had done, they had to figure out their next move. Mumbling to themselves, they headed home, anxious to park the car and the safety of their home.

Ruth suggested that they try to contact Ms. Chillicothe, apologize for what had happened, make up some reason for their actions, and plead for her sympathy, in the hope that they could mend the fences and still sell the banjo to her. Gertrude answered her daughter, that she had to be an idiot to think of trying to contact that Chillicothe person, or whoever she was, because she knew them and could finger them to the police, or worse. She paid no attention to her daughter's theory, but instead, pointed an accusing finger towards them both and accused them for the problems that existed. Then she added, this was all 'their fault,' because 'they let her escape!'

Neither Nathaniel nor Ruth agreed. They knew she screwed up, right from the beginning. It was her idea to let Appleby get involved. It had been their idea to keep the instrument in the back room where no one could find it until enough time passed, then they could sell the banjo to the highest bidder. But no, mama had to have the immediate cash!

Ruth tried to get her to change her mind, telling her that they had to stop bickering, and stop blaming each other. Nathaniel agreed with his sister when he told his mother that he thought Ruth was right. Fighting wouldn't achieve anything. They knew that Barry would like to have the stupid banjo, because their father told him he could have it, and now he wished they had let him have it!

Ruth answered that she didn't think their father should have told him that. Barry was not a direct relative, like they were. She thought they had every right to disregard their father's wishes.

Gertrude was not pleased with the way things had gone since John died! She had greed on her mind, and told her children that if their father had done as she suggested and given her the instruments in the first place, none of this would be happening now. Ruth agreed with her, but thought that since he didn't actually leave them to anyone, in writing... the only people that would have been told anything about the instruments would be those old goats he used to play with every week, Mr. Appleby, and of course, Barry.

Since it was assumed no one knew anything about the instruments, Gertrude asked why they were being subjected to an interrogation by this woman, who supposedly represented a big Eastern musical instrument company. Ruth believed that someone knew more than they did about the value of those dirty old instruments. They knew the mandolin disappeared, even before their father died. They hadn't considered that maybe, just maybe... that Barry, had inside information that they didn't have, and that maybe, he was instigating all of this stuff and might even have both of them. Gertrude scowled while telling her that she [might] be right. Maybe they underestimated this clown of a cousin, and Ben too! John could have told both of them more than they were told, about their value! Then she asked if they thought they had been taken advantage of.

Nathaniel spoke out telling them that they had not been taken advantage of... yet, and they could still hold the cards. She said that they sold the banjo to Ben, with the assumption that no one coming into his old junk shop, would consider anything of real value being there. Ruth agreed but argued that they caught the Chillicothe person at his antique shop and she must have been there for some reason, other than the one she tried to make them believe. Nathaniel became perturbed and called her a dolt! He asked her if she had forgotten that Chillicothe had waited, and then followed them there hoping they would take the bait and rush out to find the banjo.

Gertrude, with her disgusting voice, spoke up to make her point as well, telling them that they were both right, for a change. She noted that Ben said that he didn't know where the banjo was, but knowing him, he's was probably holding out for more money. The phony representative from some 'unheard of' Eastern company, followed them to Ben's place, and that's why she was coming up the walk when they were leaving. Then she asked them to consider that she was not who she said she was. The question was, why was she after those instruments?

Silence fell over the room as the three of them contemplated the situation. Each pondering a solution to the question. Who was this woman, and what did she know that they didn't know?

Like being hit by lightning, Nathaniel shouted that maybe there was something in the instruments that they wanted. He would bet that John told Barry about whatever it was, and like Ruth thought, he was probably involved in some way! Coming up with a possible answer to that question, the next one was how could they get that information from Barry, without letting him know that they are on to him?

Ruth, who had remained silent for some time, excitedly stood and told them that she had an idea.

Asked what it was, she suggested that since they agreed that Barry believed them to be snobs, why not invite him over for dinner to get the information from him. She explained that they wouldn't tell him the real reason for the invitation, instead they could say that now his Uncle John was gone, it was time to mend the fences and be a real family for a change.

Gertrude went into a frenzy with that idea being the most stupid thing she had ever heard of, allowing that riff-raff to come into their home with his long hair, probably dirty hands, and who knew what else?" She was animate about her feelings regarding Barry, and Ruth's ridiculous idea.

Nathaniel had a different perspective on his sister's idea. He asked his mother to wait a second and reconsider. He indicated it may sound insidious in nature, but they should consider it because Barry was a naïve person and they were aware of that. They also knew he wasn't a fighter, or a lover, but rather just a musician. He continued, that, after all, no one needed to know that he was there, or about their relationship, for that matter. He thought that Ruth had a good idea, and deserved some thought.

Gertrude voiced her outrage at their suggestion telling Nathaniel, they both love to annoy her. Nathaniel, hoping that his mother would forget her negativism and see the cleverness of the idea, remained calm and suggested she stop thinking everyone was against her since they were not! He suggested that when the facts were put together, Barry was definitely in the spotlight and this could be an easy way to lure the truth out of him. In his naivety, he would not be the wiser. He suggested that there must be some family tie since she did call him about the car, even if it was in an accusation way.

There was silence again. Each of them looked around the room, without seeing anything at all. If a vase would have fallen from a shelf and broke into a thousand pieces, the sound and site of it would not have kept these three from their thoughts.

Finally, the sound of Gertrude's voice interrupted the silence saying that Nathaniel was right, that she had called him about the car, because she thought that he sent someone to sniff around. Then she added that, as to his idea, she had given it some thought, before he mentioned it, of course! She said that she didn't think they would agree with her since they both wanted to attack everything she thought or said! She concluded that they should invite, not just Barry, but others too... just so he wouldn't suspect anything.

It was agreed that Ruth would make the arrangements for the party, and Nathaniel should track Barry down and make the invitation! She asked them to decide who else to invite, and she would check their list before they made fools of themselves!"

You could have heard a pin drop after her announcement. Neither of the cousins thought that their mother would agree with them; of course, when she did, it had suddenly become her idea, including an addition or two. They turned and left the room, smiling at their accomplishment, and knowing it was really Ruth's idea and the Dono house remained... in its usual disarranged order. With a plan of action, the cousins began to chart their strategy, while Gertrude bided her time while taking credit for the whole thing.

CHAPTER 15

Gertrude, with her feeling of superiority, sat by the kitchen window indulging in her daily glass of Vino Sin Juan Chardonnay. It was far from the most expensive wine, but the few guests that came to visit, always complimented her on her choice. She purchased it by the case, keeping the cost down, but the idea of an imported wine sounded exclusive. I assumed that the crackers and cheese made it palatable.

Since Barry had not been invited yet, Ruth busied herself with partial preparations. Having no experience in the kitchen, she went through the phone book in hopes of finding an inexpensive catering company, one that would consider catering to only four, or the most, eight people. After several phone calls, she found a company called, "Caterers For Hire.'

She called the number and was cheerfully greeted with Stan, the owner, asking how he could be of service. Ruth explained they were planning to have a very small, but exclusive, dinner party, to which Sam, the caterer, asked how many people the party would entail. She told him between 4 and 8 people, and he questioned the amount of people being quite small. Ruth, feeling intimidated, responded indignantly, that was what she said, four, possibly six, or eight people.

The caterer apologized telling her that it was

unusual to have so few people, and that if it were for only four, he didn't think he could accommodate her. In her spoiled and snooty voice and paying no attention to his comment, she continued by asking what kind of menus he had, and what were his rates. He responded that normally the customer told him what they would like on the menu, then feeling that his new customer had no idea of how it all worked, took a different approach and suggested that perhaps they should start by him asking her what type of meat she would prefer for the main dish.

The conversation continued for some time. Finally, after several questions and answers, Ruth was pleased with what they had discussed. The only problem was what date to choose, so she placed her hand over the mouthpiece of the phone and shouted to Nathaniel, asking what kind of a date would be convenient. Nathaniel told her that he did not reach Barry yet, so he had no idea when, or even if he was available. Then he questioned why she asked, and told her he hoped she wasn't setting up the dinner yet.

Ruth would never admit that she could have jumped the gun! She responded that she was not that dumb, to try to set something up without a date. She said that she just wanted to know, so when she set it up, she could give a date for the dinner. She removed her hand from the phone and told Stan she had a couple dates in mind, but wouldn't know for sure for a day or two and asked if she could get back to him then. Having just spent over an hour trying to work things out with Ruth, he was disgusted, but remained calm when he told her he knew how that could happen. He informed her that he would need a week's notice to fit this into his schedule and asked if he should call her later that week, or would she would prefer to call him, when she established a date. Feeling that she had been let off the hook, she told the caterer that she would contact him.

Nathaniel had a more difficult problem. The Rolodex offered no information. He could ask his mother, but that wasn't something he wanted to do unless he had no other alternative. He wondered if the old guys that played with his father might know where Barry was. Nathaniel pulled on his jacket, and slipped through the back door. There was no need to tell his mother, or his sister, what his destination was, since it was none of their business. After all, he was delegated to find his cousin Barry, and persuade him to come to the "forgiveness" dinner. Since it was after noon, and he knew the Rigby address, it seemed the logical place to start. As he arrived he heard the jam session going on. He hadn't planned on all three being there, but he figured that could be a golden opportunity. He could tell them that he was a rep from a company looking to buy an old instrument. He thought that if it worked for that Chillicothe woman, why not for him. Knock! Knock! Knock!

A kindly older gentleman answered the door and asked if he could help him. Nathaniel wasn't prepared for this nice fellow at all. I don't know what he expected, but coming from the type of family he did, he probably expected some belligerent old man with bad temperament.

Nervously he asked if he was Mr. Billy Joe. Rigby. Rigby said he was, and addressing him as 'young fella', he invited him in suggesting he should meet his friends too, then realized that he had not gotten the young fella's name. Nathaniel realized that Mr. Rigby was as forgetful as his old father had been and attempted a smile as he lied, saying his name was Sam Poole.

Billy Joe guided him into the den where the other old musicians were sitting. He introduced Nathaniel as Sam Poole. He pointed to each as he said their name, introducing them by where they sat, pointing out that the fellow in the big chair was Guy, and the fella on the couch was Tony.

Billy Joe asked Nathaniel how he got his address. He came up with a story that he got it from a clerk at the local music store, where he was hoping to find a special banjo. The store clerk told him that Billy Joe Rigby might know the whereabouts of it, since he knew that one of their group played such an instrument. The three of them listened intently, then when he was done, Billy Joe told him he might have come to the right place because they had a visitor, not long ago, that might know something about that banjo.

Nathaniel got excited and managed a more realistic smile as he asked what the person's name was and saying that he would really like to find him. The old gentlemen all looked at each other inquisitively and discovered none of them could remember the gentleman's name. They chatted between them, saying things like, was it Jim, or maybe Bill, then a "Gosh, that didn't sound right." Then looking at each other they asked if anybody wrote it down, and asked, didn't he say he was comin' back to play with us ag'in soon?

Nathaniel's hopes were dashed. The old men and their memories were lost in space somewhere, so he wasn't going to waste time with them. His voice became less than pleasant when he assumed they couldn't give him a name. They apologized, saying that they just didn't have memories like they used to. Tony tried to be as nice as he could, even though he detected a nasty change in Nathaniel's attitude. He suggested that Nathaniel leave his card, and if that fella came back, like he said he would, they'd just give him a call.

Nathaniel's face had returned to the "pouty" expression, that he displayed most of the time, as he answered that he didn't have a card with him. Having said all he felt was necessary, Nathaniel, played his final card by suggesting that fellow might be Barry, an old friend, and asked if they might know where he lived. Tony blurted out the address, but as Nathaniel closed the door, he, feeling he had done something wrong, looked at his comrades explaining that he didn't think [that fella] was very happy with them…and told them that he wasn't as nice as that other gent, the one that played with them. Then as though an afterthought, he told the other two that he reminded him of someone but he couldn't remember who.. The other two shook their heads in agreement with Tony, picked up their instruments, and resumed their playing.

CHAPTER 16

Sam's catering company was too small to have a full time staff. He needed to hire a waiter, so he called his old friend Joe, the owner of the breakfast/lunch café that I refer to as the greasy spoon. He told his friend that he had received a weird call from some chick who wanted him to cater a small, dinner party. Then he emphasized for four, maybe, seven or eight, people. Joe, who had just finished cleaning up his place and was getting ready to leave for the day, managed a short grunt of laughter as he repeated, "four people," and asked if he was kidding.

He answered that he wasn't kidding, and he hated to ask, but in the event the chick called back, would he be interested, or did he know anyone, who might be able to give him a hand by doin' the servin'. Joe told him he didn't have the time, and right off hand, he didn't know of anybody. He stopped to think and asked him to wait a sec, he did have a guy who came in every once in a while that always seems to be down on his luck. He told Sam the guy also had a real good looker for a partner, if he knew what he meant. He suggested that maybe one of them would be willin' to make a couple of bucks for an easy job.

Sam told him he wasn't too sure about someone like that, and he asked if Joe thought that one of them could handle a high society dinner party. Joe told him he thought that they could, since they were clean and neat, and just appeared to be down on their luck. He added that they had been coming into his place for a long time. Then he asked Sam if he wanted him to, he should ask them. Sam answered his friend with "Hey, why not? If you trust 'em, they must be okay." Then he added, "besides, anyone who could eat at your place, could use a job once in a while." He laughed as he ended with, "you know, for that hospital trip."

Joe was insulted and told his friend that just because he had a high-fa-lootin' place with his caterin' business, she shouldn't be too high and mighty since he wasn't calling him for help! Stan laughed off the criticism, then he apologized, told Joe he was sorry, and asked him to contact them to see if they were interested.

The sunrise, out of my bedroom window, was fantastic with the sun rising, and the light breeze coming in the window from over the lake, I decided I could just forget everything for the day and enjoy it. I stretched, yawned, and rubbed my eyes to get the night sand out of them. The new apartment was great, the case was moving along, and all was right with the world. I pulled on my trousers and padded into the bathroom to do my morning routine. I splashed on some after-shave, put on my shirt and shoes. Whistling as I left my cottage apartment, I was surprised to see Lori pull up in her car.

Her driver's side window was down so I asked her what she wanted. Lori looked like she had been up all night, and told me she couldn't sleep because she was deep in thought about our investigation. Taken by surprise, I stood staring at her before finally telling her that to be honest, I hadn't given the case a minute's thought and was considering taking the day off. She told me to get serious, we had barely broken the ice, then invited me to breakfast and told me she would buy. She practically ordered me to get in her car and she'd drive. She took me by surprise, but, without a second thought, I walked to the passenger side and got in. With a big smile, I asked what made her decide to take me to breakfast.

Of course, now being a full partner, and with women's rights, plus the fact that she makes as much as I do, why not?

She didn't answer, but rather, she drove over the causeway to the old greasy spoon and parked. We got out and ambled into the café. As usual, it was close to being empty. Joe came around the counter with two glasses of water. He grinned, forcing his cheeks to push his bristling whiskers so that they stood almost straight out from his unshaven face.

Lori couldn't resist and asked him when he was going to shave, and when was he going to get his place cleaned up.

Joe took a step back, acting as though he was hurt by her comment, the he looked at Lori, and then at me, with a stern look, he told us that he had just recommended us for a job to make a couple of bucks… but after her remarks, he wondered why. I asked what he meant by "he found a job for us to make a couple of bucks," and asked him if we looked that destitute. He said we did!

I looked at Joe, and smiled, knowing that we were all just making conversation, but also I knew he was serious, so I asked what kind of job he had found for us. He told us about the phone call he had received from Sam, the caterer. When he stopped, he started to return to the kitchen knowing that he had made the offer. Before he had taken a full step, Lori asked if the caterer told him who the client was.

Joe thought for a minute, then told us he had called his friend back, and asked if he knew who the woman was that called. He said Sam told him that his phone keeps the calling numbers, and when he checked the number, it was from a family named Dono. Neither of us could believe what we heard and asked if she told the caterer who the four, or whatever the amount of guests were. He told us he didn't ask, his friend didn't tell him, and he felt it was none of his business. He added that if we were interested, he'd let him know.

Whoever would be attending that dinner party might provide us with the information we needed. One of us needed to be there. We realized that Lori would be recognized right away by the family and Barry. Since the family barely saw me only one time, I could probably go, but Barry would recognize me. Lori suggested I could wear a wig and a mustache that would probably hide my identity.

When Joe came back to the table, I told him that Lori couldn't take the job because she had other plans for that night, but I could help his friend out. Joe beamed, thinking he had done something for us, not knowing our alternative motive.

We unlocked the office door just as the phone rang... it was Barry. He told us that he didn't like to bother us, but was wondering what progress was being made on finding the instruments. I told him we were making headway, then he told me the real reason that he called. He had received a bill for the first week's expenses, and was surprised that we had to rent a car. I explained the circumstances and told him about Lori's escapade with his relatives. He was embarrassed and told us he didn't know what to say. He was apologetic for his relative's actions. He asked if Miss Lori was alright now. I told him she was fine, still had a bruise or two from her altercation, but other than that, no problem.

He seemed relieved and asked that we keep him posted with respect to her health and closed our conversation. I barely had time to set my phone down when the landline rang. Lori answered using her undercover name. Gertrude Dono, loud and clear, was calling her. She identified herself and asked if Lori remember that she had left her card with them. Lori told her that she did. Gertrude continued to tell her that Lori had asked to call her if they found the banjo she was searching for.

Lori was more than surprised to hear from them since the attempted abduction, and coldly informed her that she remembered all too well. She continued telling her that she didn't like the sort of treatment she had received from her and her children, and her company didn't appreciate it either! Then, calmly, she asked what she wanted.

Gertrude responded in kind, telling Lori that she should be grateful that was all that happened to her since [she was following them]. She continued to say that they could have called the police instead. Lori answered that she wished Gertrude had called the police since she found that shop which had been suggested suggested to her by the motel clerk! She continued saying that unless Gertrude was calling to tell her she was sorry, and had located the instrument, there was nothing for them to talk about!

I don't remember a time when Lori was so ticked off. It was good Gertrude called on the phone and had not come by, in person. Mrs. Dono didn't have it in her vocabulary to say I'm sorry, or to apologize for anything. She had no conscience nor shame, but discovered that Lori had a tempter from time to time.

A pronouncement was made that they found the banjo. Gertrude asked what arrangements could be made for Lori to identify it, and tell them what the company was willing to pay. Lori informed her that she wouldn't be doing it at their house, and if they actually had it, and wanted it appraised, they would have to meet someplace convenient, and in public. Gertrude told her she would have to get back to her and hung up.

Lori was ready to tear the heart out of Gertrude Dono. She didn't have to tell me what the conversation was about because with both of them shrieking, I heard every word! She went to the counter sink, picked up the coffee urn, and filled it with water. I couldn't believe that she was going to make coffee, but she did. Without another word she went into her own office, closed the door, and I could hear her pacing back and forth. Suddenly she burst into the reception almost shouting that she was so mad she could bite the end off of the bumper of her car. She believed that woman had all the gall in the world and the sooner that dinner took place, the better she was going to feel!

I told Lori that I agreed with her.

Who would the other attendees be, and would we know how many? If Barry was there, would he have recognized me, even in a disguise? The old dealer might recognize me...but maybe not if I had a good enough disguise. This got tougher and tougher all the time, I wished I could have foretold the future, I hate maybes.

Lori started to rub the top of her right foot with her left shoe. She was giving a lot of thought to something and then she told me that she thought of a way to find out who the guests might be. She thought that Joe wouldn't know the date until the caterer got it from the Donos. She actually giggled, with the vision of me working there in a pair of black pants, a white shirt, a towel over my arm, and a bow tie. Subduing her giggle, she continued telling me that as she recalled, the Dono family wasn't sure where Barry was. We knew that Barry was not a favorite relative, so what if they concocted this dinner idea to make him think that he was now a part of the family, while actually hoping to get information from him? They couldn't set a date because they didn't find him yet. She asked me if that made sense of not. I nodded my head in agreement that it did.

She continued her line of thought to suggest that they would probably invite the antique dealer, not because they liked him, but because they might assume he was in cahoots with the purchaser of the banjo, and maybe, even the mandolin. In his case there would be no need to wait for a date because they already knew where he was and could invite him anytime.

I told her my thoughts about how we could learn

a thing or two. It was possible there were more people involved than we were unaware of. I was uncomfortable with our plan, not knowing who would be coming to that dinner. I told her I knew a way to find out who they were inviting. She asked me how we could do that, so I explained that Sam could tell them that he needs the names of the guests, and if they ask why, and he can tell them he includes place cards where the diners would be seated. That would give us, at the very least, the first names of the persons attending. Hopefully I wouldn't be identified by anyone there!

She agreed about the place cards, and that my being identified could completely ruin our progress, and it could be dangerous; but, that was all we had to go on…then. The big question was, could we get Sam to make the request?

CHAPTER 17

I have never liked neckties. They were too tight, I couldn't breathe, and a hundred other reasons; I just didn't like the darn things. Now I had to wear one, the caterer said so…what I thought, had nothing to do with what I wanted to wear that night... Why I agreed to let myself get set up, as a waiter at that dinner party, was beyond me... well really that wasn't true, since I hoped to learn something useful. Black bow tie, white shirt, black pants, black shoes, hair almost "beauty parlor" perfect. It wasn't me, but I'm the only one who could have done it!

Lori felt it was her responsibility to give me advice about serving, but staying invisible. She continued with the fact that I would be serving, while paying particular attention to what was being said…that I couldn't be in the room listening every minute, so that's what the little recorder, that I was going to put under the table, was going to do for us. She knew that I didn't like it, but hopefully, with the mustache, and the wig, no one would recognize me, then she got that pouty look, and apologetically told me that she wished she could have done it, but…well, I should know...then she started giggling again!

Lori's instructions, plus the orders from that ludicrous caterer, was about all I could handle. This wasn't a guy thing, it was plain ridiculous! Slipping the speaker under the table was going to be enough of a problem, let alone the rest of that stuff.

They called me Gary. Frequently loud and very clear.

What a ridiculous moniker! I don't even look like a Gary.

Gertrude called the name out, insisting they needed more wine. I answered her, with all of the dignity I could muster, "Yes mam. I'm coming."

That disgusting voice! It's Gertrude's, of course! I wanted to give her more wine, right on her lap!

She told me to hurry up, her guests were waiting, then, in an almost unintelligible voice to her guests, she apologized and called me an idiot, saying that I was slow, didn't know what I was doing, and was a complete nincompoop. Since she called me an idiot, I decided to act like one when I asked her to excuse me, and held the bottle up and asked who wanted more.

She said I was an ignoramus, and that I should be able to see whose glasses were not filled properly, and I should take care of it! She asked me where I was taught my etiquette, and then added a question, "In some bar?"

I controlled myself, but I really wanted to smack her in the mouth…just once!

Being shocked at who was there would have been an understatement. There was Barry, as we assumed he would be. Then Billy Joe Rigby, the mandolin player from the jam session, the family of course, the antique dealer, Ben Appleby, and even more unbelievable, Will Brashear and his wife, Linda. I'm sure they recognized me, but they didn't show it…thank goodness.

Nathaniel seemed to be nervous as he proposed a toast. (Now that the wine glasses were filled to the three-quarter mark.) He said the family would like to thank each of them for being there. It was with the family's deep gratitude to each of them, for taking the time out of their busy schedule. He was sure they would find the food excellent and the wine beyond reproach, then he raised his glass and toasted his father, known to most of them as Uncle John. As he raised his glass, so did the others at the table, then they took a sip of that Vino Sin Juan Chardonnay wine, which Gertrude thought was so wonderful. I couldn't help but notice the sour look on their faces, when they took a sip of that wine. It was apparent that her taste in wine did not satisfy her guest's palates.

After the toast, I served the first course, a garden salad Sam had prepared in the kitchen. The conversation around the table was the normal chitchat between people who had little in common with each other. A little politics, no religion, minor gossip that normally floats around small communities, but no mention of the instruments that I had hoped for.

The salad about finished, it was time for the second course. I was surprised that the old gal had spent the money to have Beef Wellington, but she did! Everyone appeared satisfied with that course and I had to admit it looked delicious. Finally it came time for the final course, dessert, and coffee. A beautiful crusted apple pie alamode. I got hungrier by the minute, but that desire soon disappeared when the matriarch, Gertrude Dono, stood, and addressed the group.

She started out with the comment that no doubt, they were wondering why they had been invited to her home for this dinner. I saw the uneasiness of the guests as they looked at each other, and then back at *Mrs. Doro. They all believed what Nathaniel had toasted before, to John Dono, but what was coming?*

She told them that as they were all aware, her departed husband, John, was a dear friend to all of them. Then, she spoke to her guests, raising her glass in a toast to each; to Linda and Will Brashear, the fine couple who did so much to help John in his collection efforts from past debts in his business; then to Billy Joe Rigby, the one who shared John's wonderful banjo and mandolin. She told them that John spoke of him and his ability quite highly, and he was indeed a close friend, even outside of the group in which they both played. Then she addressed Ben Appleton, who as recently as last week was an enemy, by saying that he was not only a friend to John, but also to this family. She spoke of the many hours spent with him over the past years, and how they cherished his friendship, over that time. Then, last, but certainly not least, her dear nephew, Barry, who had never been out of her thoughts. She emphasized that John treasured him, as a nephew, and that Nathaniel and Ruth had always seen him as a favorite cousin, the only other person to come and visit his Uncle John, and play the instruments with him. Then she asked all of them to lift their glasses. Of course everyone did so. There were a few grim faces and an occasional smirk at Mrs. Dono's remarks. She did well in her introductions, but unfortunately, she didn't stop while she was ahead.

She continued, saying, that in dear John's last moments, he confided in her that he would like everyone to remember that beautiful banjo, and the mandolin he played. The she said that unfortunately, through her carelessness and during her time of grief, those instruments slipped away from her home. She then asked if any of them had any knowledge of their whereabouts, would they please confide in her so they could be brought back to their proper resting place, in John's study. All of the guests looked at one another in wonder. You could tell that she was really questioning if the instruments were in someone's possession that was in attendance.

How could the Doro family

invite this group of folks, feed them wine and food,

then try to coerce information out of them?

Not surprisingly, no one spoke. Embarrassed, Nathaniel and Ruth looked at their guests. I don't know what they expected, but I think that they actually believed that with the wine, and the special catered dinner, their guests would just blurt out the information they wanted, but with their mother's last comments? While they sat there, unbelieving what had just transpired, and in a daze from their mother's request, the dinner was over and the guests left, as quickly as they could.

Once the guests had all left, Gertrude was negative, and as usual, she condemned her siblings telling them that she certainly hoped that the two of them were happy now! They had the dinner, fed everyone, gave them all wine, and she couldn't see that they gained a thing! She could not be pleased, but what she didn't realize was that she actually did something good, bringing together some folks that should have been brought together long before.

Ruth, still protecting her idea, defended the dinner, even though her goal was not accomplished since no one divulged where the instruments were. She told her mother, and her brother, that they may not have gotten a lot of information from the guests, but they did learn that Barry was searching for something, although he didn't say what. She was sure it was either the banjo or the mandolin.

She also noted that wretch of an antique dealer knew one of Uncle John's musical friends. This was interesting, since she didn't know John's acquaintances knew each other. The Brashears, who could have known something since they handled the collections for the Donos, balanced the invitation list, hopefully making it inconspicuous what the family was up to. She believed that they had opened up a dialogue with the guests, which they didn't have before. Now they knew where to find Barry, and, they also knew that he knew the old mandolin player.

Nathaniel commented that if it hadn't been for him, they would not have had the dinner at all, since he was the one who found and invited Barry! Gertrude scolded that enough was enough! She had to pay for it all and thought it was a waste of good money. She would not have been above taking credit, if it had turned out all right, but it didn't! Everything continued, as usual, with a lot of irritation between the family members. There was little learned at the dinner party but I learned how 'not to be' a waiter. Gertrude's voice still rings in my head and the caterer's voice will be indelibly etched in my memory, along with hers.

I wished I knew what I missed while I was in the kitchen.

The evening over, I drove back to my place and took off that blasted tie and the white shirt. What a relief it was when I removed the crazy hair and the fuzzy mustache. I decided to take a shower to get the stench of the Doro place off of my body. A few minutes after entering the shower, the doorbell sounded with its loud and unwelcome ring. I had barely gotten wet and now had to leave my shower? I decided to just let whoever it was, push the buzzer. Unfortunately, for me, the intruder did not stop, the ringing continued to get louder and louder. I was left with no choice, but to answer the darn thing.

I wrapped myself in a large fluffy towel, which Lori insisted I buy when moving here. I slipped into slippers. With all of the strange happenings, I moved cautiously to open the door. I turned the knob, but left the chain lock intact and opened the door slightly to see who was there.

A familiar voice emanated from the outside saying, "Well, this is a first!"

Lori told me that she didn't know I took showers at that time of night, then mischievously added, "or any other time for that matter." She enjoyed telling me what a sight I was, wrapped in a towel. Then she asked if I wanted a smaller one for my hair too, and if that wasn't enough, ended it with... "sweetie!"

I asked her what in the dickens she was doing there at that time of night. I released the chain lock and opened the door to more blustering from her about sitting in her car waiting for me. She asked if I got the recorder from under the table, and if I did, what did I find. Without taking a breath she told me she was sorry but as I had said so many times before, "time is of the essence, let's go!"

She got me. I did say that! And now I regret having said it. I knew that she was right, but that didn't make me feel any better, so I told her to come on in and wait until I got some clothes on.

She called to me through the bedroom door that she was anxious to hear what went on, and that we both needed to know if anything important happened, then she continued that I should hurry up and get dressed. She made listening to that recording sound like the world depended on our findings. I disgustedly answered "okay," hurriedly pulled on my trousers and shoved my feet back into my slippers. Shirtless, I closed the bedroom door behind me, and came into the living area where Lori was impatiently waiting to hear the recording. She said that she hoped we could hear everything that had been said at the dinner table. As we listened, there was little of value being said; then, a whispery voice, spoke quietly to John's musical friend, Billy Joe, telling whoever it was that they had to be careful if they were going to make this work, especially with those so close to him.

Billy Joe responded, quietly, almost with a whisper that he was, but it was tough with Guy and Tony. Then he said that the other person shouldn't worry since, they could hardly remember their own names, let alone anything else…then told the other party to be cautious. Speaking almost in an inaudible voice, he asked if Nathaniel reminded the other person of anyone else, to which the other fellow responded no, he didn't think so, he was just disgusting Nathaniel.

The response "that he just reminded him of someone, someone he met recently but couldn't recall a name," seemed to ring a bell for one reason or another. I filed it away in my memory to see if it would come up again, and in our favor.

Lori stopped the recording and asked me if I remembered who was sitting close to Billy Joe? He wasn't speaking loud enough for her to recognize the voice. I told her I couldn't remember who sat where, except for Gertrude.

CHAPTER 18

Just as I pushed the call button to reach our friends, Lori came into my office and asked who I was talking to. Motioning for her to wait a second or two, I waited for the phone to connect. Will answered with his usual business greeting. I told him that was a great way for him to answer, then I asked why he and Linda were at the dinner party at the Dono's. He answered by asking me what was I doing there, and with that quirky wig and mustache, then he chided me asking if business was that slow, that I had to have a part time job?

Since I asked my question first, we agreed that he should go first and told me that he and Linda had done some collection work for the Dono family, after the patriarch had passed away. There were partners that owed the company some money from a venture John had personally bankrolled. They didn't feel obligated to repay the debt, so his agency was hired to do the collecting. When Nathaniel called with the invitation, he felt that he couldn't refuse.

It was my turn to tell them what I was doing

there, serving dinner at the Dono household, but I was interrupted by Lori, who had no idea who I was talking to and whose curiosity got the better of her and rather loudly, she asked who I was talking to. Will overheard what she said and responded with a cute remark of "And how is Lori today?" I assured him that she was fine, but nosy! By then Lori guessed who I was talking to and stood with her left foot rubbing the right one again. I knew it was just a matter of time before she would be wanting to say something.

Will, now that I had averted his question for the second time, wanted to know why I was there, and in the roll of a waiter, and a bad one at that! I told him it was just an information-gathering thing that involved the case we were working on. I told him that we overheard Billy Joe, on our recorder, whispering to someone, and I wondered if he could remember the order of guests. Before he could answer, Lori snatched the phone from my grasp and again asked him if he remembered how the guests were seated. He told her that he wasn't sure, and asked why we wanted to know.

She told him a little more about our case, but didn't destroy the fiduciary bond between us and Barry. She suggested that knowing the seating arrangement could be helpful. Will told her that he vaguely remembered the seating, so she asked him if he recalled who sat on either side of the antique dealer, Ben Appleby. He asked why that was so important.

Acting like I should have heard everything Will said to her, she told him I would answer his question and handed the phone back to me. Will felt that I was there, and he made a point that since I was serving them all, I should have some memory of who sat where.

I told him that he was right, I should have. I also told him I was so flustered between the caterer yelling at me to 'take this and take that', and with Mrs. Dono dictating orders to me, that I got very confused from time to time. Will understood. After he was finished joshing me, he admitted that Mrs. Dono could be very frustrating. Searching his memory, he remembered Mrs. Dono was at the head of the table, Nathaniel was on her right, and Ruth was on her left. He and Linda were seated next to Ruth. He hesitated, and giving it a second thought, he indicated that was not right, Ben was at the end of the table, and Billy Joe was next to him and across from Barry something or other.

Jokingly I told him that those folks with the last name of 'something of other' must be proud of that name since so many people had it, and he even seemed to remember it so well. Will quickly responded telling me that he was tryin' to help us out, so I better watch it! I was certain that he smiled as he responded to my comment, even though I couldn't see him. After a few more barbs we said goodbye and I turned off my phone.

Lori was inquisitive and asked if we got any answers that were useful, or not. I told her we did, and explained the seating arrangements. She suggested that we should draw a seating chart. I felt it was important to find who was whispering to whom. It could have been Barry that we vaguely heard. She looked at me in disbelief and questioned why I would consider Barry as a suspect. I answered that it was common sense to consider that all are suspect. We have had devious clients before. This may not be the situation at all, but nonetheless, we could not overlook the possibility that we were being played. Lori had a difficult time handling that possibility, but agreed it was valid thinking.

As luck would have it, we were just getting the board prepared to make our notes when Barry showed up with his usual greeting of, good morning Mr. Deavereau and Lori, and with his hesitations, continued asking if there was any new information. Lori smiled, then told him there was nothing new, and asked how he was.

Barry smiled and sat down in one of the reception area chairs. He told us he had something new, a real surprise. Lori asked him what it was. He told us that as we knew, he didn't get along well with his aunt or his cousins so it came as a great surprise when Nathaniel invited him to a family dinner party, hoping that they could mend the fences and be a real family... for a change.

I realized that he was surprised but that didn't sound like the folks he had described to us, or the ones I met up with, either. The whole struggle between that part of the family flashed through Lori's mind, in fast-forward form.

He told us that it was really a surprise when he

met old Rigby there, knowing that he was one of his Uncle John's musical foursome. He also met some bill collectors that seemed like nice folks, even though they didn't seem to have a lot in common with the others. It sounded like he enjoyed himself, so Lori asked if there many people there.

He answered that there was, and naming them he was surprised that Ben, who owned the antique store, was there. Lori didn't want him to get into the 'Ben thing', and decided to let the guest list business drop and changed the subject, asking if the food was good. Barry told us the food was pretty good, but he sure felt sorry for the waiter that waited on them. He was like a fish out of water and didn't say much except yes mam, and no mam, to his aunt who ordered him around like a house pet!

Now we knew that he didn't recognize me. He told us about the conversations at the table, and the unexpected fine treatment he received from the Donos. What he didn't mention was, while sitting next to Ben Appleby, that any secretive conversations took place. He did tell us it had been some time since he had seen his uncle's friend, Billy Joe, and they did talk a bit, about music.

Finally he left telling us that he had some places to go, and a gig to get ready for. He said that he asked his Aunt Gertrude, Nathaniel, and Ruth to come, since it was the kind of music that his Uncle John used to like. They told me thanks, but that they were going to be busy that night and suggested that he might like to invite them to his place. He said that he told them it was much too small, but perhaps they could get together somewhere else, then Barry told us again how surprised he was that they were so nice to him. Barry stopped talking, stood, and in his usual quiet way, stepped to the door, opened it and left with a simple good bye.

Lori walked toward the closet with our whiteboard when he left, she thought we should start considering the other suspects and what their part in this might be, also, why Barry would pay us to find those instruments if he had some idea of where they might be. She felt although we didn't have much to write down, we had established who sat next to Ben from the antique store. She wrote down all that were in attendance and jotted down a few notes. She drew a brief sketch of the table seating...hoping that the way they were all seated could answer some questions later.

We needed some different scenarios, some that would hopefully give us a new look at the case and keeping in my mind Barry could be playing us. Lori jotted the actual facts we knew on the board.

1. Name: Barry Jonathan Dono

2. Address: 4004 Willow Drive, Guntersville,

3. Cell phone: 573-555-0015.

4. Relatives: Aunt Gertrude, Cousin Nathaniel, Cousin Ruth

a. Aunt Gertrude, bossy, arrogant, know it all

b. Cousin, Ruth, touchy, afraid of aunt, frightened of compliments, bitter

c. Cousin, Nathanial, afraid of aunt, but getting stronger, more aggressive, bitter   d. Uncle John-deceased

5. Search For: Mandolin, Style F4, and Serial No. 56284. 1920 Manufacture. Client claims value to be $30,000.00 According to Spurn's Guide to Gibson. 1920 shipment date. $22,000.00 Value

6. Friends: None listed

7. Acquaintances: Guy Billings, Billy Joe Rigby, Tony Schwartz
8. Occupation: Entertainer (of sorts-60's style hippie)
9. Barry invited to dinner

10. Other guests – Linda and Will Brashear, Billy Joe Rigby, Ben Appleby,Seated next to Barry-Billy Joe and Ben

11. Whispers about "being careful" between which guests?

Lori stopped writing and told me that although it probably wasn't important, it seemed odd that the old client, Sean O'Hara, liveed at 1600 Willow, Apartment #2, Albertville, and our new client lives at 4004 Willow Drive, Guntersville? Then, giving it a second thought, she said that one was in Albertville and the other in Guntersville. Since we had never physically drove by either of those addresses, we considered that we might be being duped by these two guys.

That was an interesting theory and it was time to go for a drive and check those two addresses out…I didn't know why I didn't do that before then, as we generally checked out these things in the beginning..

My first thought was to drive over and check it out, then Lori suggested we check it out with google instead driving over there. I looked at her like she was someone from outer space, then it dawned on me that she was right, we could do it all on the computer, faster and without any expense. She sat down at her computer and pulled up the information. The address in Albertville was a go, but the address in Guntersville was bogus. There was a Willow Beach Road but no Willow Drive.

Why would Barry give us an address that doesn't exist?

It was my idea to call him on his cell phone and ask to meet him at his place. We could tell him that we found something we didn't want to discuss on the phone. Lori liked the idea and suggested that she make the call, rather than me, because in her opinion he saw her more of a secretary than an investigator. She fingered the number. No answer. To be sure she entered it properly, she punched it in again. This time it rang and Barry answered. She told him who it was and realizing it was short notice, we needed to come over to his place because we had some new information that couldn't be discussed on the phone.

I couldn't hear what the response was, but Lori did that foot thing again and that let me know that she was either thinking about, or was unhappy about, something. Closing the call, she told me he said the place was a bachelor pad, not well kept, and the landlord was in the middle of a remodeling project so it would be best to meet him somewhere else. That sounded like a cop-out for sure. How wrong were we to not have checked this out before? Now we had another thing to be concerned with.

Why did he give us an address that could be so easily checked out?

CHAPTER 19

A breather was needed so we decided to forget the case for a while. The address problem was plaguing us both and we needed to sort it out without Barry thinking we had reason to mistrust him. I suggested that we go to my place, since it was a bit bigger than her tiny apartment. She agreed. We parked in front, I unlocked the door and held it open for her. She was enthused by the way the place looked. Probably the fact that she helped me pick out the furniture and décor played a role in her enthusiasm.

Sitting in the kitchen, she had a nice view of the living room. Inquisitively, she stood and pointed at a long, cardboard box in the middle of the living room floor. Being as busy as I was when moving in, I opened it partially and was so surprised at what I saw I didn't open it any further. Now Lori was there, and I had no alternative but to show her what was in it.

She asked me why I didn't tell her about it before. I probably should have told her that I was so surprised I just closed it back up again and haven't opened it since. Lori wanted to know where it came from, so I told her I didn't have a clue since I never took it out of the box. She removed the wrapping paper and started to remove the object from the box. Her eyes bulged and she told me that she had never seen a 'blunderbuss' that close before, it must be an antique! Being careful is something you learn quickly when you find something unexpected, so she checked under it for a wire, or some other indication that it could explode. A note slipped out. I hadn't noticed it before so I picked it up. It read, "I always thought that you needed a bigger gun. I found this one in the old store, under the floorboards...maybe you can use it. (ha-ha), Regards, Joanne."

Lori was infuriated to think that I was keeping a secret. She said that she thought Joanne went back to Florida! Her face was flushed. She was not a happy camper and started rubbing that right foot with her left one again. That made me nervous! I looked at her with the most caring look I could muster, and told her that Joanne Birdsley did leave several months ago, and I had no idea how that box got into my stuff.

She was upset and sarcastically told me that things just don't show up, out of the blue, and there must be quite a story behind the gift. I told her to forget it! Joanne was long gone and how that box got into the old apartment was beyond me, and besides, we had more important fish to fry.

I was hoping that she would settle down. As I recall, she was the one who told me to find someone my own age and have some fun, which I did. Then Joanne went back to Florida...at least I thought so.

At last she slowed down and agreed that I was right and that it was none of her business, continuing that Joanne had been my friend, just like Linda and Will, and she knew that affair was over a year ago. She wiped away a tear that had started running down her cheek, and told me that she was sorry. I felt like a heel. I knew better than to console her, because one thing could lead to another... besides I try to think of her as a daughter, or maybe a younger sister.

I asked her if I should put on a pot of coffee or fix us a drink of something. She told me that she would rather have something else... if I didn't mind. I reluctantly agreed with her, fearing what that could lead to. She wanted something with a little 'oomph' behind it to settle her nerves. I fixed her a vodka gimlet. It had a smooth and almost sweet taste. She had never had one, but she liked it. I fixed one of my double shots of good Lismore Single Malt with a spot of water, plus a couple of ice cubes for myself.

We both were mentally exhausted. The case had taken a nasty turn neither of us expected. We felt certain that Barry and Sean had to know each other. They were about the same age, both had lived here, and nowhere else. One was clean cut and worked at the bank, and the other clean, but more hippy in appearance. Barry liked his freedom to go where the music took him. Maybe Sean liked that scene as well. Could they have the music in common, or could it be the places Barry played in.

Maybe we were both mentally pooped and jumping to conclusions? Maybe what we both needed was a night out!

I asked Lori if she would like to have a night out and she surprised me, agreeing that would be a pleasant change. There was rarely anything going on in Guntersville, and even less in Albertville so we decided to drive up to Huntsville. We didn't need to change clothes since everyone went casual. We locked the door behind us and climbed into the Olds. The usual, we turned on the key, there was one backfire, a puff of blue smoke, and we were ready to rumble.

We made the leisurely trip through the mountain passes along side of the Tennessee River. The beauty of the trip itself helped us both to relax. It took us about forty-five minutes to reach the city, and another half hour to find a place that looked fun. We found a place called Reggie's that had food, drink, and karaoke, plus it advertised live music… It was just what the doctor ordered.

A very attractive young lady, in a skirt that seemed almost too small for her, escorted us to a table. It was not too close to the stage, but close enough that we could enjoy the entertainment and our meal. She asked if we would like a drink while the food was being prepared. I suggested that maybe we should get a glass of water, but Lori felt one more drink wouldn't get us into too much trouble. I had a draft Bud, and she decided to have something wild, which surprised me. She ordered some kind of an exotic sounding beverage and it came with a straw, a little umbrella, and looked like something out of the bartender's handbook. She took a sip and told me it was delicious. We sipped our drinks, waiting for our dinner when the entertainer stepped onto the stage. To our surprise, it was Barry! He was accompanied by a drummer, a clarinetist, and a keyboard player. He couldn't see us, since the lights on the stage practically blinds the entertainers. We were impressed with his arrangements, and his singing as well. I noticed that there were no hesitations in his vocalization, like there was in his everyday speaking.

We listened to the group, forgetting for the moment that we could, somehow, be his victims. We enjoyed our before dinner drink and almost too soon, our meals were brought to the table. We ate like two ravaged beasts on the verge of starvation! As we were ordering desert, the karaoke host took the stage. He asked for someone to come forward, and several people turned their heads away, hoping that their eyes would not meet with his, ushering them onto the stage. He did a solo from an old Sinatra album that enticed some of the more courageous to come forward. We were mesmerized by the atmosphere, the entertainment, and the evening. We ordered another drink or two and reveled in the intoxication of the night. Neither of us payed particular attention to who came to sing, that is until one of the participants caught our eye. It was Sean

O'Hara!

He stopped at Barry's table. We could not make out what was being said between them and thought it best if we left, but my nasty habit of listening to things I was not supposed to hear gnawed at me. I excused myself to go to the restroom, and carefully made my way through the diners to a place where I could hear most of their conversation, without being seen.

It was just small talk. Sean told Barry he didn't know that he played so well. Then he asked what made him come all the way up to Huntsville to play and at the same time asked if there wasn't somewhere in Guntersville or Albertville that he could get a gig in. Barry answered that it wasn't that easy, if you were in your own hometown, no one appreciated you. He told him he gets a lot of gigs over in Scottsboro and also in Gadsden, but at home…practically nothing. Sean suggested that he ought to be in Nashville because that's where the money was. Barry shrugged his shoulders, and told him that was probably true, but they wanted guys that wear tight jeans, big hats, and move around like they have ants in their pants…that just wasn't him. He told Sean he liked to feel the music, and loved the old songs; then he told him he had written a couple of songs but discovered that he was living in the wrong century.

Sean knew that Barry was doing something that he liked to do, while he was stuck in the bank five days a week, and sometimes six. Same customers day in and day out, and each one of them double checking everything he did 'cause they thought he might be short changing them. Sean was not too happy with his lot, maybe a bit envious of his newly met friend. Sean smiled at Barry and told him that at least they wouldn't have to do things, they didn't want to, forever.

They continued their conversation. It appeared that Barry had found a confidant. He told Sean about the instruments his uncle John said would be his one day. Sean questioned him about the special mandolin, explaining that he collected old things too. He told him about the check he had just recovered.

They appeared to be getting 'too well' acquainted. It sounded to me as though they had just met. Two guys, too much booze, and discouraged with their own lonesomeness. I was concerned with the comment by Sean. "At least we won't have to do things, we don't want to, forever"

I edged through the crowd, back to Lori, who was keeping time to the music with her foot. She asked me what took me so long, and I told her the place was busy, I had to wait my turn. We finished our drinks, left the place, and headed toward Guntersville. It was dark so I stayed alert for any wayward deer that might dash onto the highway! Fortunately, we arrived safely at my place within an hour.

Lori told me that she didn't want to drive home and asked if she could stay at my place for the night. She was slurring her words and trying for my sympathy, told me that it had been forever since she did anything but work, and she wanted that evening to never end. I didn't want to agree with her, so I told her it would be best if I took her to her place. She responded that she would like another of those "whatevers" I made for her earlier, and just cool it with some of my CD albums. (she knew I had a filled CD rack). I lowered my shield of concern, and cast my good sense to the wind. Lori and I both were too tired and too wrapped up in this case to think clearly.

Time to get up came earlier than I would have liked. I was shocked to discover that I wasn't alone! Last night was undoubtedly a mistake. We were both embarrassed at our lack of judgement, and didn't say anything to each other on the way to the office. The rest of the morning went by without much discussion. Lori seemed a little distant, and I hoped it had nothing to do with last night. She gets that way when we are not making the headway she expects, so hopefully she is deep in thought about the case. I went to lunch alone, at a different place than usual, closer to my apartment. On my way back to the office, another driver, not paying any attention to what he was doing, cut me off in his hurry to pass me and get back into the proper lane. I hit the brakes causing my car to slide sideways and up against the curb.

When I got back to the office, I rushed past Lori toward the bathroom, hoping that she wouldn't notice, but as luck would have it, with the drying blood on my cheek, and a bulging face under my eye, she easily saw that something had happened.

She asked me what in the world happened, and if I had an accident. I hated to tell her about my brief loss of control, but decided to tell her, that on my way back to the office, and not paying attention to my driving, a blue sedan pulled in front of me. I jammed on the brakes and skidded sideways, ending up with my left front wheel against the curb. I guess the shock got me disoriented, because the next thing I knew, a big hulk stood by my door. He didn't look too happy. I can't say that I was either, but what I didn't need was some wise guy yelling at me for something that he caused. I rolled down my window. Wrong thing to do! Before I could say a word, his big fist came through the air and hit my right eye and the side of my nose. The blood spurted, and I was mad. Second nature took hold and I opened the door slamming it against him hard enough to knock him down. Before he got up, I was on him like a coyote on a rabbit and busted him in the mouth; he fell back to the ground. I knew that if I let him up, he'd probably kill me, so I stayed sitting, with my knees on each side of his chest. I pulled back my right arm, acting like I was going to bust him again, and asked if he wanted another one or if he had had enough! He put his hand in front of his face and asked me to stop, shouting he was sorry.

As I was afraid she would, Lori called me a dummy, and started the spiel about my not knowing when I start thinking too much when I am driving, that I don't see everything I should! Then, after cooling down, she told me I was lucky I didn't get hurt more than I did! Finally she asked about damage to my car. I told her there wasn't any, so she asked about the other guy's car. I told her that I didn't notice because when I let him up, he jumped into his sedan and left. Then she asked if there were any witnesses. Hoping to end the interrogation, I looked at her and told her not to sweat it!

I cleaned myself up and put a cold washcloth on my eye. Lori was waiting for me with a hot cup of coffee in her hands. Calmed down, she asked me if I was alright, and told me she was sorry she yelled at me, then she asked if she could look at my eye. She told me I had a nasty bump and was probably going to have a black eye to boot. Finally she settled down and I told her that wasn't my first trip around the block and probably wouldn't be the last.

She waved her hand back and forth in front of my face and asked me if I was awake since we had a case to solve. Her pushy attitude shattered my thoughts. Reality took hold, and I rejoined the world of the conscious. I told her I knew we had a case, thanks for the help on the eye, and assured her that next time I wouldn't be so absorbed in thought when I was driving.

CHAPTER 20

The next few hours we used the computer to search for information on each of the people we had been in contact with since the beginning. Some interesting facts came up. Some that we didn't expect! We had no idea that Barry's father was named Frank and he was still around, or that he had a half-sister named Mary Joseph. A bigger surprise that his dad had remarried to a Madge O'Hara...like in Sean O'Hara?

Barry Dono:

Age: 28,

Name at Birth: Barry John Dono,

Father: Frank Joseph Dono, Mother: Anna Maria (Christensen) Dono.

Sister: Half-sister, Mary Joseph (Dono)

Name changed legally eliminating Dono

Education: Guntersville High- University of

Alabama, Majors English and Music-Did

not graduate Profession: Musician

Criminal Record: 2015-Petty Theft- filed by Jason's Music Studio-(Sheet Music, Guitar

Picks.)   2016-Assault – Filed by Mary Joseph – No conviction

Marital: Single

The theft was foolish. Who would try to steal sheet music or picks for an instrument? Those were penny ante things that anyone could afford to buy. Why would anyone risk their reputation over such a trivial thing? As to the assault arrest, I wondered about what that was really about. Never heard of Mary Joseph before, and her name wasn't in the mix.

I asked Lori to run a check on Mary Joseph suggesting that whatever we uncover could have a bearing on our case!

>   Mary Joseph – Age 33 – Born Mary May Joseph Dono
>
>   Father: Frank Joseph Dono –
>
>   Mother: Madge (O'Hara) Dono
>
>   Education: Willow Point High –
>
>   Profession: Waitress, Helen's Bistro
>
>   Criminal Record: 2015 Theft - filed by Jason's Music Studio-Huntsville - Stolen Instruments –

Personal:Married Aug 2012-Divorced Sept 2016.

Now we had an added perspective. Barry and Mary had Jason's Music Studio in common, and they had the same father. Barry never told us he had a half-sister, or that they had a physical altercation. I wondered what that was all about.

While I was busy with my research on the computer, Lori did some legwork. Since she had gotten along so well with the shop owner, Ben Appleby, she decided to go for broke! She parked, on the side street, in good visual contact with the shops large window. As she was getting out of her car, she purposely let her skirt ride a little higher than usual. As she had hoped, the door opened and Ben came out to... sweep off the stoop? He almost dropped his broom, in his urgency to greet her. He greeted her with a "Good morning miss, isn't it a beautiful day? What brings you to see me today, still looking for that special instrument?"

Lori smiled and answered that it could be because one never knew what they may find, and it could be something he had. Ben smiled back, and held the door open for her. She thanked him and told him he was a gentleman. He answered that he tried to be, and told her he was just having his morning tea, would she like to join him. She accepted his invitation and asked for two sugar cubes in her cup. He told her that he was quite spoiled and always had some real cream as well. Lori told him that she liked cream occasionally. He beamed with enthusiasm, probably dreaming not only of the lovely young lady he was having tea with, but even more, thinking about some great sale he might make.

After idle chitchat, Ben stood and asked her what she was looking for this time. Lori uncrossed her legs, and stood up, re-adjusting her skirt. Ben couldn't help but pay more attention to her actions than what he was doing and bumped into a table with some crystal displayed on it. One piece crashed to the floor and broke into pieces. Embarrassed he asked her to excuse him while he got a broom and dustpan to pick the mess up with. He scurried off to the back room. While he was gone, Lori took another look at the various displays in the hopes that she might find something that could be a clue to Billy Joe's [quiet conversation] with him the night of the party. She found nothing, and Ben returned too quickly for her to check everything.

Asking if she could help, she squatted to hold the dustpan. Apparently not many of his customers were this attractive and Ben, trying to keep his eyes on the mess he had created, swept the broken pieces into the pan. He told her he had forgotten her name and she reminded him it was Judy, Judy Chillicothe, and asked if he now remembered. Asking how could he forget her, he asked her to forgive his old man's memory. Lori winked at him flirtatiously and she would forgive him, just because he was who he was.

He was so overwhelmed with her beauty, and now her slight flirtation, that he would probably have given her anything she wanted. She took advantage of the situation and told him that she had been in contact with some old cronies of John Dono, and they had mentioned to her that he also played an instrument. Ben looked at her and smiled, admitting that he did, and now she knew his secret.

She responded that she didn't know his secret, then she did her foot thing. He watched her curvaceous ankle move back and forth, almost hypnotized by the motion. He caught himself, and the ruddiness of his cheeks radiated embarrassment as he knew he had a special interest in her…all of her, and knowing that she was aware of his enchantment with her.

Ben told her that he didn't play well, but did try to play the mandolin. The other fellows, in that group, didn't care much for him, so Billy Joe and he were trying, cautiously, to convince them to accept him. Since their mutual friend, John Dono left this world, he hoped that they could overcome their discomfort with him and let him play in John's place. He and Billy Joe hoped to come up with a plan making it possible for him to get into their good graces.

Lori acted concerned, when she told him that she understand, and told him that her company was going to send another rep to find that special banjo she was seeking, but at the last minute they decided that the fellow was a too starchy for small town folks and she should remain there. She frowned in her pouty way, plying for some pity, and hoping Ben would shed some light on the banjo's whereabouts. She whimpered and suggested that if she went back empty handed, she would never live it down.

Ben went back to his chair and sat down and asked her to come and sit at the table again. Lori joined him where they had drank their cups of tea. She could feel that he was about to see things her way, and she told him she knew he said he hadn't seen that special banjo, but asked if he was sure about it. She continued saying that it was really an unusual piece, something he couldn't forget.

He broke down, and in confidence told her that he hadn't been honest with her. He could see that she could be in some trouble if she went back to the city without that banjo. He told her that John Dono's widow sold the mandolin and a banjo to him! He figured she was just getting rid of John's stuff since she had no interest in anything he had, except his money. He momentarily stopped telling his story to ask if she would like some more tea. She said no, so he continued, telling her that he gave Mrs. Dono what he considered a fair price at the time? He continued that was about the same time that Billy Joe and he started talking about him takin' old John's place with the group. He knew if he showed up with that mandolin, he would never be accepted by any of them so he told her that he found a buyer for it, but the fellow wanted to trade-in another instrument of far less value. He told him that he'd sell it to him for $2,000.00, plus his old mandolin, and he accepted the deal, his name was Sean, or something like that.

Lori asked him if he knew where she could find him. He told her to sit still while he checked his record book because he was sure that he had the customer's name and address. Ben called out the address from across the room, and she wrote it down. His name was Sean O'Hara and he lived at 1600 Willow Street in Albertville, Apartment 2. Lori thanked him, and left, giving him a peck on the cheek. His face turned a bright red and he felt that the smile probably would never leave his face, as he followed her to the door and watched as she got into her car and drove off.

I was still working on the computer when she returned. It was all she could do to contain her enthusiasm. She had found the mandolin! The only problem was, no mention of the banjo was made.

Was it possible that Mrs. Dono only sold Ben the mandolin, and not the banjo? We were halfway home, but still weren't close to the home plate. Where could the banjo be? What did the Dono family do with it, or more to the point, what did Gertrude do with it?

CHAPTER 21

We added the new facts about Sean and Barry, as well as the assumed location of the mandolin. Now that we knew where it was, we wondered if we knew as much about Sean and Barry as we originally thought we did. I admit that was puzzling. If they were no more than acquaintances, which they appeared to be at the club in Huntsville, why would Barry tell Sean about the instruments? Sean was a Roosevelt artifact collector and a bank teller, neither of those interests had much to do with music.

More and more it seemed when we found an answer, it posed more questions. We decided to talk to the Donos again. Gertrude had already contacted Lori using her undercover name of Judy, and asked her to meet her. Then she re-contacted her to tell her where to meet. I suggested Lori call her back, and make her believe that she had to leave town in the next couple of days. Hopefully that would cause a reaction that could help us wind up this search. Lori agreed.

Mrs. Dono answered, which was unusual as the trivial business of answering phones and doors was generally left up to Ruth. She asked who was calling. Lori told her it was Judy Chillicothe, and reminded her that she was to call her with a meeting place and time. She told Lori that she didn't get the banjo and that's why she didn't call.

Lori tried to sound as respectful as possible, telling her that she was so sorry and that she had hoped that they could meet and resolve the situation. She told her that she was being called back to the office and had to be there in two days.

Gertrude, concerned she was going to lose out making some money, told her that was a shame, and that if she could just stall the company for a couple more days, that she was sure that she would have the banjo. Lori told her that it was doubtful she could stall returning to the East, but she would try.

Lori told me that now, the ball was in Gertrude's court. I suggested that she, using her car, and not renting another one, follow Gertrude because there was a chance a close surveillance of Gertrude's movements might shed some light on where she thought the banjo could be. It was a gamble, we thought that we knew where the mandolin was, but the big money was still on the other half of our search.

At least we could write off the Appleby/Rigby connection. I hoped, for Ben's sake, they would find forgiveness and he would be musically accomplished enough to fit in.

I'd like to have known what the beef was between Ben and the other two guys, but probably it wasn't important. It was something not worth worrying about and none of my business.

Thinking that a stiff drink of my good scotch might be alright since it was almost three o'clock in the afternoon, and since Lori was busy doing surveillance work, I decided to take a physical look at Barry's address. I drove to my apartment, pulled into my parking spot and discovered Will's car parked next to it. He came out of the manager's office as I started up the walk. He asked if I had a minute because he had some rather interesting information for me. I told him that I always had time for an old friend, even a scotch... if that old friend was interested? He told me it was too early for him to have a drink... that made me feel guilty.

Will told me that Sean told him a story about someone had purchased a mandolin from him and gave him a rubber check. He asked the agency to help him recover his money. Apparently, Will asked him how much money, and was told a couple thousand bucks. When Sean said that, Will remembered the conversation we had when I told him that I was searching for a couple of instruments. He thought that could be one of them!

I told him it very possibly could be, and asked if he had an address on the mandolin guy. He told me he did, and that was where he was going and wondered if I would like to go with him, because he might need a little back up. I went straight to my bed stand drawer where I kept my .45 automatic. I slipped it into my jacket pocket, checked for messages, and returned to

Will. Since he knew where we were going, he drove. He filled me in on his collection efforts, and the closer we got to our destination, the more excited I became. When we pulled up in front of the address I recognized it at once as being the address that Sean had given me when we took his case, 1600 Willow. I told Will that this address supposedly was Sean O'Hara's.

Puzzled, Will told me that couldn't be because it wasn't the home address that Sean gave to him. I continued to insist that it was the address Sean gave us. We slipped out of the car and quietly closed the doors. The front door to the cottage was slightly ajar. I reached into my jacket pocket and retrieved my .45. Will carefully pushed the door open a little further. The light came in through the window and we could see the body of a young woman on the floor. Her watch and necklace picked up the sunlight, but that was all that was visible from where we stood. Will stepped back from the open door and suggested that we call the cops.

I didn't need any trouble and agreed with Will. This was not someone that passed on from old age, it was a young woman, and moving anything at all could get us involved.

I told him I'd call since I had my cell in my pocket, but Will pulled out his phone and pushed the emergency button. He told them he was Will Brashear, and he was at 1600 Willow in Albertville. Keeping it short as possible, he told them he came to make a collection call and found a body.

In minutes two cops arrived and went into the building. We could distinctly hear the call being made from one of their shoulder phones. "Yes, it's on the floor in the living room. What? No, of course we haven't touched anything." Then the dispatch told him that an investigator would be right there, to secure the scene and let no one in! It was less than five minutes when they arrived, two plain-clothes cops. They told us their names were Officer Flynn and Officer Conner. They ordered us to stay where we were, then they went into the room and checked the body for a pulse, there was none. They discovered a purse on the couch. We could easily hear their conversation as they read off the name of Mary Joseph from her driver's license.

I couldn't believe it. I wondered if the photo on the license matched the body. Why is Mary Joseph, a half-sister of Barry's, at this address, and in an apartment supposedly belonging to Sean O'Hara?

Both of the officers knew us, but as a matter procedure they checked our I.D.s anyway. I asked if she had been shot, and they confided that she had been stabbed, in the neck, with an unknown object that punctured her left carotid artery. They told us we were free to go, but wanted us to come down to the station in the morning for statements. We assured them that we would do that, then we left.

Will was as shook up as I was. He took me back

to my apartment and we both had a scotch! After Will left, I returned to my office and told Lori what had happened. I asked her how come her observation was over so quickly. She explained that the Dono family never left their home. They had one visitor that Lori described as over six feet tall, probably 200 pounds, had sandy colored hair, a mustache, and a small goatee. He appeared to be around 50 years of age, more or less.

I asked if she got his license plate and she told me that she did. The plate was a special-order plate with the initials of FJD. Immediately I knew it was Barry's father. One thing was certain! He could not have been in two places at the same time, so he was off the hook for the puncture wound in the neck of his daughter, Mary Joseph.

We added the new facts. A murder has been added to our board. We wondered how this daughter of Frank's could be involved, especially with Sean O'Hara... I called Detective Sergeant Johnson hoping that he might fill in a few blanks. I might as well not have called! He was tighter than a clam regarding the questions I had for him. He made me feel like I was the murderer. So much for that! I got back on the computer and did another search on Frank Dono.

Name: Frank Joseph Dono

Address: unknown

Education: Albertville High

Occupation: Corporate C.E.O., Auto Mechanic, Karaoke Host, Waiter

Criminal Record: Embezzlement, Assault with a deadly weapon, Parole Violation

Personal: Divorced from Anna Maria (Christensen) Dono-deceased

Current Wife: Madge (O'Hara) Dono

Daughter: Mary May Joseph – now deceased!

Son: Barry Dono –

We didn't know why Barry preferred to not be connected to his father, but what about his mother, Mary. How did she die, and how? Sometimes these records are not complete, so I ran the mother through our search engine and re-established that she was deceased. Her death was listed as a "Cold Case," and had been left open for several years. Lori didn't like where this was going, originally it was a 'search and find' case for a guy that seemed pretty up and up. Now she started to question whether he was legit or not. She asked my thoughts, since she had become more deeply concerned with the case hour by hour.

I felt pretty much the same way. First it was just to locate an instrument or two, then we discovered that the Dono family was less than straight with us, and seemed relentless in their effort to find the instruments when they discovered that we were searching for them, and they may be valuable. They went so far as to attempt kidnapping Lori. We had a murder that must have some direct relationship to our case! It didn't appear that Barry had been honest with us. We felt the need to interrogate him hoping for more facts if we were to shed any light on this screwed up mess!

Lori called him telling him that we had run into a snag and needed him to stop by and clear it up for us. He was soon at our door. He didn't knock, but came in smiling a smile that fit with his long bushy hair. He asked if he had come fast enough and we answered that he did, and offered him something to drink. He told us no thanks, but thanked us for the offer. After some minor chitchat, it came time to get down to business so I started the questioning, hoping to find some answers.

First I asked why he didn't tell us about his dad. He told us his dad just wasn't a person he wanted to be associated with, so I asked him, "Why not?" He told us that his aunt had to raise him, because his father was a bad man and in prison. She also told him that his mother had gone to heaven, unexpectedly!

I asked him why his aunt raised him and now doesn't seem to care for him to be around. Barry told us that she thought he just wanted to be with his uncle and get his money. I asked him if he knew what gave her that impression. He got nervous and asked for a soda. Lori went to the refrigerator and grabbed a Pepsi. Barry took a sip, then thanking Lori, he continued telling us that his uncle used to tell him about a bright future that was ahead of him, and that he was going to be well-off someday.

We told him that with the talent he had, we had to agree with his uncle. I took a sip of my coffee, (which was on the verge of ice-coffee) then I told him that there seemed to be no reason for his aunt to feel that way, so I wondered if there was anything to really backup his uncle's comment.

It seemed that he was starting to get uneasy with our line of questioning and he told us that he really didn't want to talk about the past. I decided to push harder so I told him that we knew about his half-sister, and about his dad's past too. It was understandable about his hesitation to tell us, but if any of them might be involved in the instrument disappearance, we needed to know about it. I left it open for him to comment, in the hope that he would give us something to go on. He didn't. He told us he didn't figure his family was relevant in finding the instruments so I asked him what caused the altercation between him and his half-sister, Mary Joseph, in 2016.

He told us that it was really nothing. She told him their dad wanted her to have Uncle John's banjo. She screamed at him, and he lost it and slapped her. He got arrested and hadn't seen her since. The case was dismissed since she did not show up for the trial. It wasn't important anymore. We told him it was relevant now, because his half-sister, Mary, had been murdered. Barry, almost dropping his Pepsi, looked at us with his mouth gaping open in disbelief, as he exclaimed, Mary is dead! He acted like that couldn't be true. I had to ask him if he thought that his father could do anything like that. Barry, still in disbelief, answered that he didn't know him at all, but could not believe he would do anything to his daughter, especially the one he thought should have that magnificent instrument.

Lori asked him why he gave us a bad address, one that didn't even exist. He took a deep gulp of his Pepsi, then he sat the bottle on the side table and told us that we had the wrong idea. They were building an apartment building there, and it wasn't finished. He told us his apartment was done and they allowed him to move in, but it wasn't in any directory yet.

We thanked him for his honesty, then asked how many people knew about that instrument, giving him a lot of 'yes and no' answers to speed up the inquiry. He acknowledged a new friend, Sean had been told something about it when he met him at a club in Huntsville.

I asked if he thought that his half-sister might have tried to find the banjo her father told her about. He answered he didn't think so, she was new to the area and would have no idea where to look. Then I asked a pointed question about whether he had considered, that with his dad's track record, he might go after those instruments, after all, he was your uncle's brother and certainly knew the value of them. Lori suggested that maybe the death of his half-sister had nothing to do with the instruments, but questioned why his half-sister's body was found at Sean O'Hara's apartment.

He answered that he didn't think those things tied together, since she had dropped the Dono name. Sean would not have thought about any family relationship. Then he added that besides, he had just met Sean in Huntsville, and he seemed like a nice guy.

I considered going further by asking about any knowledge of his stepmother, but gave it a second thought, thinking that might be a long shot. We decided to let up on him a little. We told him that he was right. There was no way that he could have known you were her brother, unless, she told him. Unfortunately, we didn't know what the connection was between Sean and his half-sister. Sheepishly, he answered that none of us, or at least he, didn't know the connection, if there was one.

I asked Lori if she had anything else that she wanted to tell, or ask, Barry. She said she didn't.

Barry finished his drink in one gulp, then stood and with a tear in his eye, he told us this was a mess and he wished that he hadn't started to search for those instruments. Lori tried to comfort him by saying that we never knew what would happen when a search was started. In a perfect world we would run down a few leads, get the information we needed, and find what we were searching for. Everyone would have been pleased that the item was found. This just wasn't one of those times.

She asked him to not discuss what we had uncovered. He shrugged his shoulders and nodded in agreement. As was his nature, he said nothing more, just got up and left. Lori started writing down the new information on the board:

Mary Joseph was killed for some reason.

There was no rape suspected, at least for now. Certainly theft wasn't a motive, since Mary was wearing a necklace and still had her wristwatch. It seemed doubtful that a thief would have left anything that would have been of value.

Why was she in Sean's place, and where was Sean?

Have the police found him yet, and if they had, what did he say?

Did he really just meet Barry for the first time, or did Barry lie about that or could Sean been involved with someone else?

Barry was too shaken with the news about his half-sister to have been involved, or he was a very good actor! He told us about meeting Sean without our badgering him.

Who else could have been involved? Was it someone in the Dono family, or maybe one of Barry's acquaintances in the music business?

Why did Sean have the mandolin, or did he really have it at all?

CHAPTER 22

I wondered if it was time for us to let the people, that we had been cautious about, know who we really were! We had been playing cat and mouse with them for some time, and the only one who knew who we really were was Barry. I thought that if they knew who we were, it might have been a successful "scare" tactic" that could have paid off.

Lori looked at me with that inquisitive expression, then started massaging the top of that right foot again. She finished writing what we had learned on the board and put the sharpie down; then staring off into space in a world of her own, she asked me if we did what I suggested, could we have forced them into being more secretive than they already were?

I understood her concern, and argued that maybe that could happen, but that I thought they'd get nervous and think that we knew a lot more than we were letting on. When that happened, the guilty party would start making mistakes that, until then, hadn't been made.

She said, okay, let's say you're right. Which one of the suspects should we approach first and asked if I had figured that out yet. I answered that we should start with the three jam session members. She agreed.

We pulled up in front of Tony's place just as the other guys were leaving. The timing was perfect. We said hello and good-bye to the two of them as they departed, and were welcomed by Tony as he held the door open to let us in. He asked what he could do for us, and after a second or two, added the name Bud. I told him no, I wasn't really Bud, and then explained why I had called myself by that name. I re-introduced myself as Bill Deavereau, and Lori, as my partner, and told him that we were trying to locate a banjo and the special mandolin that had belonged to John Dono. Tony took a deep breath, trying to absorb this new information, then asked why I hadn't told him who I was in the first place. It was tough explaining the ruse, but he seemed to accept my explanation.

Tony looked up at me from his chair, and asked what he had to do with any of it. Lori told him that we felt that if everyone knew what we were looking for, the instruments could have been sold to the wrong people, destroyed, or hidden somewhere forever. Whoever had them knew that they were stolen. Tony nodded and agreed that could be a problem, but he still didn't understand what he had to do with all of it.

I explained to him that we had been trying to meet and investigate everyone that our client was associated with. As it happened, he was on the list of members in the music group, and that it was just plain luck I had come to investigate on the night the whole group was there.

He understood, so we told him that we didn't

want to scare him, but, recently, I and another detective, found the body of a young lady that possibly had some tie-in with these missing instruments, and that although we didn't know what that was yet, we did know that the investigation had become dangerous to anyone who was, or might have been, associated with the instruments.

He asked if that meant he could be killed, or something like that. We thought he was becoming frightened, but instead his eyes lit up and he asked how he could help. We explained that was why Lori and I came out of the "under cover" phase of our investigation, so we could get some help, we could use his help, but we couldn't tell him that it wouldn't be dangerous.

I gave him as many facts as I could, starting with the dinner party at the Dono home that we believed they gave in hopes of finding out who had the instruments. Your friend, Billy Joe was there, and the newest member of your group, Ben Appleby was also there.

Tony questioned whether or not we were sure of our information, and asked what Billy Joe had to do with it. He looked at the wall and then at us, with a bit of disgust in his voice, he asked if he invited Ben to replace John.

We divulged what we knew about Barry, John's nephew, being there, and that we figured that he was invited because he was his Uncle John's favorite. It was our thought that Gertrude assumed he could have the instruments, since before John died, he told her that his nephew, Barry, should get them. We knew that they did not give them to him when John died, but instead, allegedly sold them to an antique dealer, which was Ben. We think they thought Barry found, and then hid them.

Lori explained her role in the earlier contact with the Dono family, telling them about wanting to buy John's banjo for a company in the East. That was why they, using the dinner, tried to reign in all of the people that they thought might have some knowledge about the banjo and the mandolin, hoping to get both instruments back, and make a profitable sale.

Tony, sat poised on the edge of his chair. He had his ear glued to the conversation and didn't miss a word. He looked at us for a minute, then put his hand on his chin as though stroking a beard and told us that he wanted to help us. He told us that Nathaniel came to his place, pretending to be someone else claiming he too, was a representative of some company, and asked about that same banjo.

His eyes fell to the floor as he told us that John was his best friend and that the group were all pleased that Barry had become the great musician he had become, and if Barry was supposed to have those instruments, he was in!

We outlined what we thought he could handle, by suggesting that being a friend of Billy Joe's, and now a closer associate of Ben, that he should pay attention to their conversations. We needed to know if they were friends before, and what their involvement was, if any. He agreed to listen intently and let us know. We were aware that he wanted to vindicate his friend, Billy Joe.

We were confident that he wouldn't tell anyone about our meeting and would welcome Ben, as the new jam group partner. That could mean that Ben's unknowing accomplice, Billy Joe was also being used, but hopefully, it would prove that none of them were involved?

Next stop, the antique store. We parked in the parking space beside Ben's store. We walked up the short drive and went inside. He didn't see us through the window from where he watched from the comfort of his chair, but when we entered the store, he greeted us like old customers gushing as to how wonderful it was to see that we were still around, but although excited to see us, he seemed confused to see Lori. She flirtingly told him that we were still around, but we had a confession to make. Jokingly he asked what she was confessing to and questioned what we were going to tell him. Then he fantasized that maybe we were both really concert musicians and were there to buy my best instruments.

We told him we were sorry, that would have been nice, but unfortunately, not true. Lori told him who she really was and introduced herself and me, explaining we were not who we said we were earlier. Bewildered, Ben sat down and stared at the floor. He asked what he had done and asked why we were there. Then, with a sorrowful look, asked Lori why she had lied to him.

I started the interrogation with Ben, by informing him that we were hired to locate two instruments; a 1920 Mandolin and a banjo with the Indian Headdress on the back of it. I explained that Lori posed as an official with a company, out East, in the hopes of getting a substantial lead on the whereabouts of these items. He was being investigated because he was identified as a friend of John's, an acquaintance of Gertrude's, and as a dealer that could have contacts to sell those instruments to.

Ben looked up, like a disobedient puppy and told us that he did buy the banjo, but because of his friendship with John, and his dislike for his wife, Gertrude, he decided to keep it hidden away until the time was right that he might offer it to John's nephew…at a reasonable price of course.

I could see the thought that went into this plan, and it made sense. I asked him when he expected to offer the banjo to Barry. He was caught off guard, finding that we knew Barry, and he asked if we knew him well.

Lori was a bit tenacious when she answered, telling him that Barry was such a nice young man and a talented musician, that she didn't understand how he could have taken advantage of his friend's death like that!

In self-defense, he answered that it wasn't like it

sounded. He explained that before he contacted Barry, he had hoped to play it with John's old group. That chance didn't arrive until the other night when he attended an unexpected dinner at the Dono home. It was there that he encountered Billy Joe, a mutual friend of John's, and they started talking about him and the others. After some conversation, he asked if I would like to play with them. We were lucky to be sitting close enough to talk, while Barry was daydreaming about something else. I suggested that it was necessary that no one heard us, and he agreed that the less anyone knew, the better off we were, since I was no longer a favorite of the group.

Lori was a little more understanding, but still not satisfied and asked him again, when he was going to let Barry know he had it. He told her that he couldn't answer that because he was falling in love with the instrument himself, and that made it harder for him to let go of it. Especially since he finally had the chance to play in John's absence.

It was my turn to ask the questions, so I asked him, now that he had played it, how soon was he going to, at least contact Barry. He studied the question a while, then said that now that the cat's out of the bag...before he could finish his sentence, Lori interrupted him asking if he would consider letting us take it to him. Ben flinched at her request and asked why he should do that.

As usual, she was prepared with a long reason and told him that for starters, he wouldn't want Barry to know that he had it all of this time and didn't contact him. Next, since we had been hired to find it, and we did just that, we should be the ones to take it to him, eliminating any discussion how we obtained it, and then, going into another direction all together, she threatened him suggesting to him that if he didn't give it to them she was certain that the group would not take kindly to his joining them permanently.

Feeling the vice closing around him, he told Lori, that since she put it that way, he had no choice, so if she'd just sit still for a minute, he would get it for us. He did.

I looked at her in disbelief. I couldn't believe that she threatened him, even though he had it coming. It was doubtful that Ben would be cut from the group anyway, since they needed a fourth player; but, he didn't know that.

He returned with the banjo in its carrying case. We both wanted to see what this instrument looked like so we removed it from the case and gasped at the beauty of the thing. It was indeed a 'one of a kind.' Lori put the banjo into its case and closed it. I watched as a tear came from Ben's eye. I guess that he knew he did the right thing for his old friend, John, although it pained him to give the banjo up.

We took the banjo, and after saying goodbye to Ben, I put it on the back seat, and locked the back doors. We listened for the backfire and saw the burst of smoke and headed to our office, where the banjo would remain until we solved the rest of the mystery.

CHAPTER 23

We had to find Sean O'Hara. We knew that Mary Joseph was found in his place but no one seemed to be able to locate him. Lori was convinced that he was in the middle of all of this, but I still wasn't too sure. He was less than forthright with information, but the address that he gave us was right, although everything else was wrong. He should have had some belongings there, or some other clue about his whereabouts that should have surfaced after Mary Joseph's death, but during the police search of the place, there didn't seem to be anything. We decided that I should call Sergeant Johnson again. We might get some information that would be helpful to us, if we were lucky!

He answered with his usual decorum of Detective Department, Sergeant Johnson. How can I help you? As soon as I spoke, he knew who it was and informed me that I should know the rules there, then continued with, he assumed that I was calling about the recent murder that took place in O'Hara's place. Lori, listening on the other phone, whispered that I should agree with him, so I answered that was right, that he had been a client, and I was wondering if there was anything that he could tell me about the murdered girl, or if he might be holding a suspect.

Abruptly He answered that he couldn't tell me anything about the girl, that was privileged information in an "ongoing investigation," and repeated that, I should know that, then continued that he had no one in custody, and if he did have, the suspect would also be part of an ongoing investigation.

I told him that I thought just this once, he could tell me something, since I have another case that might be entangled with this one. He closed off the phone, ending our conversation with, "Sorry Bill." Lori heard the conversation and told me I probably should have known better, since when Rob was on duty, he was 100% cop!

I racked my brain for the name of someone else who could help and remembered my friend, Dr. Vale. She was the county coroner and could tell us how the girl was killed, if she was raped, and anything else that could be of value.

. The operator asked who was calling and I told her my name was Bill, and that I was a friend of the doctor's. The doctor answered and asked again who it was that was calling, so I told her Bill Deavereau, and asked how she was doing. She told me to cut the crap and asked what I wanted, admonishing me that to her knowledge, the only time I called her was when I wanted something. I whined that she hurt my feelings, and asked if she remembered, that I had called a while back, and I didn't ask about any cases. That's when she dropped the bomb telling me that was true. I, instead of asking about a case, had asked her what kind of poison a person could use that was not detectable.

She was right! I apologized, then explained that she had a corpse whose brother was one of my clients. I needed to know, for his sake, whether she had been beaten and raped. She said, surprise, surprise, that I knew that was an ongoing investigation and she couldn't tell me anything. I leaned a little on our friendship in the past, hoping that for [old time's sake], she would give me information that could I could pass on to her brother, to ease his pain. Trying to be cute, she told me that she was under the impression that we just went out and found things for clients and she didn't know we were murder investigators as well. Ignoring her question, I rambled on about the guy that was supposed to live where Will and I had found the girl and that I was just 'back-up' in case of trouble since Will didn't want his wife along, not with the baby and all.

She asked, if it was Will's client, and I was only helping him out, why did I want the info? I tried to explain that the guy's place wasn't being occupied by him, that he was acquainted with my client, and that was why Will asked me to go along with him. We didn't expect to find a dead Mary Joseph, and as I told her before, she was the sister of my client.

She finally gave in and told me this one time she would help. Mary Joseph was stabbed in the left carotid artery with an object like a ballpoint pen, but that hadn't been substantiated as the weapon yet. As to rape, "No." As to other information, she couldn't give me any, but she hoped that the information she gave me would help, then concluded her call telling me, don't call her again about an ongoing investigation.

Lori was eagerly awaiting the news so I told her that Valerie told me Mary was killed with some object like a ballpoint pen, and, she wasn't raped. That was all I got from her, then I added that most folks aren't killed by a ballpoint pen, unless it's fatigue from writing too much.

She thought the joke was uncalled for, and thought we should cut the jokes and try to figure out if this info was going to help us or not. She dutifully entered the new information on the whiteboard, along with the deceased name, and for a lack of a better residence, she used Sean's address. Time was running out and we still had a lot to discover. I felt we were fortunate to learn what we did, but I was uncertain as to how it would help us. We needed to find Sean and had no idea of how to go about that. We decided to call Will to see if he had any leads that we could follow up on, since now it appeared our cases were becoming attached to one another.

I called and asked him how he was doin' and remarked that was some mess, wasn't it? I told him that Lori and I were still investigating and found out that Sean purchased a mandolin from the antique dealer, that we were trying to locate for our client, then I asked if he had heard any more about Sean or where he might be found. He told me that he had some information, but it wasn't squeaky clean, since it came to him anonymously. He asked if I had a pencil and paper handy. I answered that I did.

He told me to write down 4471 Mountain Way, and he told me that it was supposed to be the last known address of Sean. He had just received the information from one of his informants. I understood and asked if he had gone there yet, and he told me that he had not, because he just received the information about ten minutes before I called. Since he indicated that he couldn't get up there until the next day, I suggested that Lori and I go up and be sure it was a good address.

Will put his hand over the phone, I assumed he was talking to Linda. When he removed his hand, he told me that Linda and he agreed that was a good idea, as long as we didn't tip our hand so he might disappear again. I assured him that we would be very cautious, and if we were spotted I'd say that we were in the area, and decided to stop by and see how his Roosevelt collection was growing. We would be very careful, especially since the last person that may have talked to him was dead.

I wondered why the police couldn't find him...maybe the confidante' was only loyal to Will?

The trip up the mountain was always beautiful. The rock, the squirrels, and birds, even that unexpected deer crossing in front of the car, all made it spectacular. Lori enjoyed the trip, as much as I did, and maybe that had something to do with us following up on a decent lead.

The address was only a stone's throw from Will's place and I pondered the question of why Sean would get a place, practically next door to someone he was being investigated by.

I parked down the mountain, a short distance from the address. There was more than one cottage located there, so we didn't look suspicious as we walked into the area. We found the address Will gave us and made our way to it. Lori knocked on the door. No answer! I decided to knock louder. I knocked so hard a small trickle of blood, caused by a splinter on the wood, ran across my hand. Still no answer! I told Lori to stand back, I was going in and didn't want her to get hurt. I braced myself to get a good push! It wasn't locked and opened so easily I fell through the doorway, and landed on the floor. There in front of me, lying face down, I found Sean. I checked his pulse. There was none, but did see a small hole, almost crusted over, on his neck. It looked like the same killer had struck again!

`I got up to my feet, brushed off my clothing and told Lori to stay outside and call 911 to report some guy was not answering his door and give them the address, then hang up.

What we didn't need then was to become suspects.

Quickly, Lori removed her phone from her waist and pushed the emergency icon. When they answered she repeated what I suggested. Thankfully they didn't have time to track the call. We left as quickly as we could, without arousing any suspicion. All we needed was to be seen speeding away by some nosy neighbor. Lori called Will, as we drove away, and told him what we found.

I didn't like this at all, but maybe we were getting closer to our goal…finding the mandolin.

CHAPTER 24

We had eliminated Ben, the antique shop owner, Mary Joseph, who really wasn't a suspect in the first place, Sean O'Hara, the collector, and hopefully old Tony. We didn't take Billy Joe Rigby off our list, since I was still curious about why he invited Ben to play in John's place.

Deciding to call on Billy Joe Rigby, this time at his home, I punched the icon for phone, and called Tony, hoping to get his address. He asked who was calling and talked very quietly, as though someone might hear him. Discovering it was me calling, he asked if we needed him yet; he was ready to help us. I assured him that we couldn't be overheard, and that seemed to relax him a bit. His nervousness was unnecessary, but I understood his concern, considering his age and all. I told him I needed the address of his friend, Billy Joe Rigby. He asked what I wanted it for, then in whisper he asked if he was the bad guy and wondered if he had to be careful with him.

I assured him that he didn't have to worry. I wasn't going to tell anyone where I got the address, and besides I didn't think Billy Joe was guilty of anything. That seemed to settle him down so he gave me the information that I needed.

Lori investigated any connection that might

exist between Billy Joe and Sean. While she did that I traveled the short distance from our office to the address Tony had given me. I walked around the front of the car, and I noticed what I assumed to be Billy Joe's car, with a convertible parked beside it. Being cautious became necessary, so rather than knock on the door, I decided go back to my car to wait and see who his visitor was. I didn't have to wait too long before someone came out, and it wasn't Billy Joe. I waited until he got into the other car and left.

I knocked on the door and Billy Joe answered, asking me how I was doing. I answered I was well and suggested that I wasn't sure if he remembered me or not. He asked me if I brought my guitar and could play a bit. I was surprised that he remembered me, and more surprised that he wanted me to come in and play a set. Maybe I was barking up the wrong tree! Not wanting to divulge my identity just yet, I told him that I didn't have my guitar with me but had just come over to chat. He welcomed me in and said we could just josh a bit then.

He stepped aside, with the screen door in his grasp, and I walked pasted him into his house. I told him he had a nice place, that I could see he had a lot of musical paraphernalia on the walls as decoration and suggested that it must have taken a lifetime to collect it all. He told me that as a matter of fact it did take almost that long because he had started when in his twenties and just couldn't stop collectin'. My memory was being tested as there were several posters advertising different entertainers from the country western shows, some instruments that were probably no longer playable, and even some outdated sheet music, some from as far back as the 30's. What a collection, and I hoped to remember as much as possible.

Asking if he had more of these things than were on his walls, I was hopeful that he would tell me that he had more and would show them to me, of course I was hoping to see that banjo. He looked around at his collection, then told me that was it. He had it all on the walls. He told me that he had asked John for his instruments, when he had no more need for them, but was told that the instruments were going to go to his nephew, Barry.

I thought if I was cagey enough, he might tell me who had left, just before I came in, but I wasn't cagey enough when I asked him if he had many visitors these days. He answered not too many. Mostly friends he'd had a long time, like the fellas he played with. The added that he don't know if Ben would become a part of the group or not, though. He told me that he and Ben went back a long time but he didn't always trust him. He did invite him to fill in for John, 'cause regardless whether he liked him or not, he was a pretty good musician, and since I never came back…

I told him I was sorry about that, but my hand hadn't healed up yet, and I didn't want to just come over there and sit for 'who knows how long'.

He told me he forgot his manners and asked if I'd like a cup of coffee, or something. I didn't need any more coffee since I had already drank more than I should have, and since I wasn't getting anywhere, I decided to let him in on the truth. I told him my real name and explained that I had a client that wanted me to find the mandolin, and the banjo that John had. He confided that I wasn't the only one lookin' for those two instruments. He said that John's son was just there asking about the very same thing. Tried to make me believe he was a fella named Sam Poole. The he called him a darn fool.

Billy Joe was surprised that I knew the Dono family and told me that not many folks care much for them. He continued that he only let that young fella in, just before I came, because he told him that Barry sent him. Billy Joe said he figured Nat was lyin' to him, he didn't figure that family had told the truth since they were brought into this world!

Thanking Billy Joe for the information, I told him he was okay, and I was glad to finally tell him the truth. I was sorry that I had to check on everyone to get the information I needed, and then I told him to watch his back. He asked what I meant by that, and wondered if he was in danger.

I felt it was necessary for me to forewarn him, and explained that in the last couple of days, two persons of interest had been killed, and that made it necessary. He was amazed someone would hurt someone over a couple of old stringed instruments. He told me they had to be over 50 years old, and asked who'd want 'em.

All I told him was that whoever was out there, was dangerous, so he should keep his door locked, and he shouldn't let anyone in he didn't know and trust!

Walking to the door to leave, I felt a strong hand on my shoulder. I instinctively turned around to face whoever it was. A sign of relief took hold of me as Billy Joe, with a big smile, took my hand and shook it. He thanked me for the information and told me if he heard anything he thought I ought to know about, he'd call me. He asked for my business card. I left, feeling confident that Lori and I had another new friend, and hopefully another one that can help us solve the case. He had a much stronger hand than I expected from a man his age, probably due to the hand exercises one gets with all of the pickin' those guys have done.

Now the list had narrowed down some more. There was still the Doro family on our suspect list. I wasn't comfortable with them being there. While they no doubt were the most irritating bunch I had ever met, and while they did try to kidnap Lori, they just didn't seem bright enough to pull something this deadly off. Greedy they definitely were, and maybe for a buck, they'd go to extremes, but murder? Just seemed to me there was still something missing. I didn't think that Nathaniel had the guts to go any further than he did, in trying to find the instruments.

CHAPTER 25

FJD? Frank Joseph Dono, a man that we knew little about, until recently. We weren't sure what we knew other than he was Barry's father and that he had a wife who had passed away, a second wife who wasn't much to write home about, and a daughter who had just been murdered, and as of yet, no known reason for her death. We needed to get all the information on Frank Dono that we could. It seemed strange to me that no one mentioned his name before, including Barry, until we pressured him. The best bet was to try for an address.

I called Barry and was told he had no idea where his father was. He told me that it's doubtful that his father would contact him, since they have little to talk about. He was adamant about it!

Lori came into my office and told me she did a newer search, using one of the search engines we pay for. It did a complete background check on Mr. Doro.

Name: Frank Joseph Dono

Age: 61

Marital Status:

First Marriage – Mary May Joseph, deceased, reason unknown

Son: Barry Dono – Age 28

Second Marriage – Madge R. O'Hara

Daughter: Mary Joseph (Dono) – name changed, dropping Dono

Origin: Caucasian – 3rd generation American

Occupation: Mechanic

Criminal Background: Embezzlement

Current Address: 1312 West 9th Avenue- Willow Point, Alabama

Current Phone: None

Employment: CEO, Dono Investments (implicated in embezzlement-found guilty) Car mechanic,

Lori, after getting this information, felt a definite need to see what Frank Dono looked like. She was also curious to see if Madge was still in Willow Point as well. She suggested that we take a trip to find out. I agreed, because I too, wondered about this Madge, the second wife. Barry had not mentioned her either. His lack of telling us the whole truth was annoying. Determined to have more information before we confronted this Frank character, I felt we should run a check on Madge. After some bullying on my part, Lori agreed to run the check, as long as we were going to meet them face to face.

> Name: Madge R. (O'Hara) Dono
>
> Age: 45
>
> Marital Status: Husband: Frank Joseph Dono
>
> Daughter: Mary Joseph (Dono) last name not used
>
> Relationship: Brother, Sean O'Hara
>
> Origin: Caucasian
>
> Occupation: Beautician
>
> Criminal Background: Perjury, child endangerment, theft, prostitution
>
> Current Address: 1312 West 9th Avenue – Willow Point, Alabama
>
> Current Phone: Unlisted

Now we had a more complete picture. We could have sat there all day and came up a dozen theories. It appeared that at least they could be in this together… what [this] might be, we weren't certain of at that point. After several calls to some business associates, we discovered that they were staying in a temporary 'motel' of sorts in Arab, instead of in Willow Point. We decided to bite the bullet and take a trip to Arab, after all it was just over the hill, less than 20 miles from our office.

It was a short time before we arrived at the outskirts of the town. We soon entered the long street going into downtown Arab, following it until the right turn-off took us away from downtown. After a few more blocks we made a left turn onto 9th. This was a rundown part of town, but we had anticipated that! A few blocks and we were there.

It was a ratty looking place that should have been painted years ago. The white paint was chipping off in several places, the eaves trough hung loose on one end, leaving the downspout bent in the middle and what remained of it, laying on the ground. It didn't look like it should be occupied, but some seedy landlords collect the rent, do nothing to maintain the places they own, and for the most part, probably lose as much as they gain, due to non-paying transients who just disappear into the hinterland.

I got out of the car and checked my .45 to be sure I had put ammunition into it. I seldom take it with me. I felt checking it before going to visit Frank Dono was a good judgement call! I told Lori to wait in the car until I gave her a sign it was safe.

I made my way up the broken cement walkway to the front door of 1312. Looking back over my shoulder to be sure Lori was alright, I knocked on the door. At first there was no answer, then someone moved the torn drape from the front window, just enough to see me. I waited to see what would happen next. The door opened a crack. I could see the safety chain fell into a loop and was attached to the casing.

A man's voice asked what I wanted. I asked if he was Frank Dono and he, in return asked who I was. I flashed my identification and answered that I was private detective Deavereau. He said he didn't know me and asked what I wanted, so I told him I was working with his son, Barry. There was silence for a moment or two, then he said, he had not seen his son in years and asked me why he would want me to find him.

Knowing that the woman who opened the door could close it, I stuck my shoe in the space between the door and the door jam and told him, I didn't drive there to be ignored. He told me I wasn't a cop and he didn't have to talk to me if he didn't want to. He inferred that if I didn't move my foot he was going to call the police!

Before she could kick my foot out of the way and close the door, I threw my shoulder against it and broke the chain lock. I was inside faster than he could get out of his chair, and I pushed my hand against his chest.

He looked like someone I had already met so I told him that he looked very familiar, and asked why that was?

Frank looked up at me and grinned. He told me he saw that I still had a bit of a black eye. He added that when he got up I was going to have another one.

I took a second look at him and realized that he stood about six foot two and probably weighed in around 220 pounds. Taking a second look I recognized him as the same hulk I had the altercation with earlier that week with the car episode. His size gave him a bit of an advantage, except, he had had a drink or two. I didn't want any trouble and didn't think he did either. Fortunately, for both of us, he sat back down in the chair that looked like it couldn't support a five-pound sack of flour. I remained standing; then I felt a presence behind me.

I turned around to see a thin, old before her time, woman standing in the doorway holding a snub nose .38. She had it leveled at my chest and suggested that I better not move. She told me that she could use the gun pretty good and wouldn't hesitate a minute to use it on me.

No sooner had she threatened me, than Lori, who had gone around to the rear of the house, entered through the back door, put her weapon against the back of the woman's head, and told her to put her weapon on the floor, and place her hands on her head. The woman knew she had lost control of the situation and did as she was told. While never taking her gun off of her, Lori kicked her revolver to the side of the room and told the woman, to take a seat in the beat-up chair beside Frank.

Now that things were in our favor, I told them I needed to talk to both of them. Lori remained standing and never flinched. She held her weapon on them like a pro. I know this was the first time she had even attempted to use it. I told Lori to keep both of them covered.

I told them again that my name was Bill Deavereau, and told them to call me Deavereau. My partner was Lori. I felt that was all they needed to know about us. I told them that we were working for his son, Barry, and we needed some information. I asked again if they understood... and they both shook their heads that they did.

I continued, asking if he was Barry's father and also John Dono's brother. He nodded that he was.

I stated that he also had a daughter, Mary Joseph, who dropped the last name, and again, he nodded in agreement.

Then I inquired as to why she didn't want to use her real last name and was told that was none of my business.

Apparently he hadn't heard that she had been murdered, so when I told him it seemed to be a shock!

Questioningly, he looked up and told us that he didn't know about his daughter's death, and asked what had happened. His wife never changed the expression of anger on her face.

Not offering any more information, I asked why they were in Arab. Acting cocky he told us he liked it there. I wanted to punch him in the face so badly, but I knew that wouldn't help me get the answers that I wanted so I asked if there was a reason he wasn't in contact with the family for so many years. He told us that they just didn't get along, he had his ways, and they had theirs. They got the money, and he got the jail, so they didn't have much in common.

I asked him what kind of instrument he played and he asked if he looked like someone running around playing instruments.

He called out my name (leaning pretty hard on the 'Deavereau' part) telling me that what happened in his family wasn't any of my business. Then he asked again about his daughter's murder. I answered I couldn't tell him about that, because I could not get any information out of the local police in Guntersville, but I could tell him that I had to pry the information about him out of his son.

I suggested that it was a tough deal, not knowing Barry and now losing his daughter as well. He responded that Barry didn't need him because he was maintained by his brother who probably spoiled him rotten with music lessons, sending him to college, and who knows what else. He also told us that he had not seen his daughter in years, but the news of her loss was devastating.

I turned my attention to the woman and asked if she was Frank's wife. She answered that I if I didn't know the answer to that, I was a lousy detective! We were now certain, this had to be Madge!

I told her it was apparent that she was a few

years younger than Frank and asked if he had been a good provider. She bellowed back to me saying he was a lousy provider, and using more foul language told me to go to hell. I suggested it appeared to me that she must have already been there. Of course she became unglued and shouted that they had what was supposed to have been a one-night stand, but he knocked her up and so they got married. She guessed that she was the first broad he found after he got out of prison.

I pressed on asking if Mary was her child. She answered she was, but it didn't matter because she was on her own, and had been since she was 16 years old.

Lori started that foot rubbing business again. It was only a few minutes before she came a step closer to the couch, and looking directly at Madge asked, what relation she was to Sean O'Hara. Madge seemed to be shocked to hear the name, Sean O'Hara, and answered, "Girlee, that's none of your business."

Before I could stop her, Lori took a step closer and pushed her .38 against Madge's head. Infuriated, she told Madge to not use that crap on her…her name was Lori, and if she was too stupid to pronounce it, she would be glad to teach her how!

Not to be intimidated, Madge answered loudly that where she'd been, Lori wouldn't stand a chance, and gun or no gun she didn't scare that easy, so she could just stick it!

Lori wasn't prepared for that. She went as far as

she dared. I thought at the time that temper rarely comes out, and thank goodness it subsided.

I decided to take a different tac, so I told them both, look, we aren't getting anywhere, so here is the way it's going to go. Looking at Madge, I told that that I knew that she was in parole violation. I needed information they weren't giving me, and that I would ask them both a couple more questions, and either they gave me straight answers, or I'd take out my cell phone and call a friend of mine at the Guntersville Police Station, a Sergeant Johnson that might like to talk to her, if not both of them.

They sat there a few more seconds. We watched as they looked at each other, then I asked them if they wanted to talk to us... or to him. Begrudgingly, they agreed to talk to us.

We spent another half hour with the two of them, and found out that before Frank went to prison, he had a drinking problem. While in prison, he did some tax work for the staff, and some of the prisoners, and at the same time was taught the basics of automobile mechanics. After getting out he became a drunk and was fired as car mechanic.

Prior to his incarceration, he had worked with his brother. When the money started coming in from their investments, he was accused of embezzling a substantial sum of money form the firm. They arrested him, but since he was only in his early twenties, they gave him a light sentence of a few years. He knew of his son, who, after his incarceration for the embezzlement, and his wife being killed in an accident, was sent to be raised by, John and his wife Gertrude. The untold part of that story was that Gertrude did the embezzling, and framed him, but has continued sending him money from time to time without anyone's knowledge while at the same time depleting Barry's inheritance.

The problem was much the same as we all have read or heard about; a young guy is put into prison with seasoned criminals. Trying to stay in one piece, he gives in to the pressure and becomes one of them. After he gets out, the family doesn't want him around and he is thrown to the wolves.

Now I knew why Barry had little recollection of the truth. It was never told to him, and his mother never had the chance to know or raise him. Gertrude's greed overtook what decency she might have had. Now, what about Frank?

The two of them had quieted down so Lori put her gun away. Madge was no different, but we noticed a change in Frank's attitude, and his apparent unhappiness with Madge. I decided it was time to leave, dropped my card on the kitchen table, and told Lori we should go. I told them we would be in contact with them again...soon.

On our way back to Guntersville, we stopped at the Holiday Inn restaurant on the river for dinner, and after a drink and good food, we decided to call it a night. We didn't discuss any further what had transpired, and decided to try and relax.

The next morning we met at the office. Lori told me she had entered all of the new information on the board, but it seemed to her that the more we found out, the less we knew. I agreed with her, something still wasn't right. Instead of adding suspects, we have eliminated one and added one. The thing that caused me to add one and delete one, was that Frank didn't appear to know about his daughter's death, but it seemed like Madge might.

Could this all be a fragment of my imagination? Could Madge kill her own daughter? And what about Sean, her little brother?

Client 1.

1. Name: Sean O'Hara. - Irish decent.

2. Worked at Brown National Bank.-Cashier

3. Single- has no family, (see correction)

> Discovered to have father, Frank Dono; Sister, Madge O'Hara; Half Sister, Mary Joseph Dono; Mother Madge O'Hara

4. Sings in a quartet - Brandy's Place.

5. Home address, 1600 Willow, Apartment 2, Albertville."

6. Reason for choosing us: We found counterfeit plates for Oliver Best

7. Now discovered to have purchased banjo from Ben for $2,000.00

8. Has been murdered

Client 2

1. Name: Barry Jonathan Dono

2. Address: 4004 Willow Drive, Guntersville,

3. Cell phone: 573-555-0015.

4. Relatives: Aunt Gertrude, Cousin Nathaniel, Cousin Ruth, Uncle John-deceased

    Also half-sister; Mary Joseph Dono

5. Search For: Mandolin, Style F4, and Serial No. 56284. 1920 Manufacture.

    Client claims value to be $30,000.00 According to Spurn's Guide to Gibson. Shipment date; 1920

    Value $22,000.00

6. Friends: None listed

7. Acquaintances: Guy Billings, Billy Joe Rigby, Tony Schwartz, Sean O'Hara

8. Occupation: Entertainer (60's style hippie)

Facts for Client 1

1. Mandolin, collector's item stolen. Expensive. Check O'Hara

2. Banjo, Also collector's item. Check out antique shop and owner, Mr. Ben Appleby

3. Dono Family, apparently sold banjo to Appleby

4. Lori's undercover name – Judy Chillicothe

5. Lori's undercover company - Golden String Gallery of Cincinnati

6. Bill's undercover name – Bud Anderson

7. Uncle John's group- Guy Billings, Billy Joe Rigby, and Tony Schwartz

8. 8. Occupation: Entertainer (-60's style hippie)

Incidents

1. Barry invited to dinner at Dono Family Residence
2. Other guests – Linda and Will Brashear, Billy Joe Rigby, Ben Appleby
3. Seated next to Barry-Billy Joe and Ben

4. Whispers about being careful between no longer a mystery

New List of Suspects (Also Barry's relatives unknown at this time)

Name: Frank Joseph Dono

Age: 61

Marital Status:

  First Marriage: Mary May Joseph, deceased,

    Son; Barry Dono – Age 26

  Second: Madge O'Hara

    Dhtr: Mary Joseph

Origin: Caucasian – 3rd generation American

Occupation: None Listed

Criminal Background: Embezzelment-Child Support

Current Address: Mayflower Motel-Unit 1312-Arab, Alabama

Current Phone: None

Instrument of Death

Name: Madge R. (O'Hara) Dono

Age: 48

Marital Status: Married

Husband: Frank Joseph Dono

Daughter: Mary Joseph (Dono) last name not used (now deceased)

Brother: Sean O'Hara

Origin: Caucasian

Occupation: Beautician

Criminal Background: Perjury, theft, drug abuse, prostitution

Current Address: Mayflower Motel – Unit 1312 – Arab, Alabama

Previous Address: 1312 West 9th Avenue- Willow Point, Alabama

<u>Other</u>

Mandolin purchased from Appleby by Sean O'Hara

Sean O'Hara murdered

Banjo – In our storage.

Mary Joseph (Dono) Murdered

Lori told me the board was as up to date as she could make it. It was apparent that we should look at the whole picture, as confusing as it might be, and hopefully come up with something.

I didn't have a great answer. A lot of people were involved that made this more mysterious than normal. Of course if it wasn't, Barry wouldn't have needed us.

Lori said we should try to start at the beginning, or at least what we considered the beginning. There was Sean, the bank teller, who came to us to find a lost check. We decided to vent about Sean, even though he was dead, we might put something together that made sense.

We showed up in the right place and at the right time to see Sean and Barry together. They seemed pretty buddy-buddy, and Barry's explanation wasn't that pat. It did seem a little strange that Sean could be a 1950's or 1960's music type.

Lori was doing that foot thing going again. Her opinion was that Sean collects old things, so that type of music, being old school, might be a better fit than we thought. She still was leaning toward Barry telling the truth, so I let it go. We moved onto Barry himself. If his uncle and he were so close, why didn't the uncle, in his last days, and on his deathbed, call for Barry and give the instruments to him? Could it be they weren't that close after all?

Her consideration was, if that was so, why did the family treat him like they did. It seemed to her that they might have been more lovey-dovey with Barry, since they despised John so much. I had to admit she had me on that one, but, maybe they don't like any relative that might be in the way of them getting what they felt they deserved at the time of the will reading, especially if Barry was thrust upon the old bat to raise, when the real mother died. Just sayin'.

Lori had another thought. What if there was something hidden inside of one, or maybe both of those instruments that was much more valuable than the instruments themselves? Maybe bank notes, or bonds, or maybe even bearer notes? Maybe another will? I had to agree that thought had merit. So, agreeing that she had a point, I had to question why the two murders? Why did Frank suddenly arrive on the scene? Why, a little earlier, did Sean seek out Barry, or did he? I never thought about that but it made a whole new thing out of it, didn't it?"

Under Facts, she wrote, See if hidden treasures are possible. We continued down the list. Of all the people we had met, the insane family of Dono took the prize for ignorance, arrogance, and just plain wickedness.

We both agreed on that one. But, using logic, they knew nothing of the value, or even thought about it, until she called on them. That's when we discovered that they would do almost anything for a buck.

Lori said that may be true, but as nasty and inhospitable as they were, and as low as they might go, she didn't see them as murderers. She knew they tried to abduct her, but if they were really killers, she doubted that she would still be there. I had to agree!

My theory was that they over-reacted. They knew they did something wrong and the minute they saw her, their fear took over and they acted spontaneously. That's where their ignorance came into play and when they lost it! Lori, instead of rubbing the top of her foot, took off her shoe and threw it at me and yelled at the same time, that was a spontaneous act!

She missed me and I laughed. She stared at me for a second or two, then she began laughing too. Tears rolling down her cheeks, she told me I was bad, then hummed that old song about bad, bad LeRoy Brown. In her imagination she could still see me in that ridiculous wig and false mustache I wore at that dinner party. That memory was funny as her throwing her shoe…and missing. We both laughed like nitwits over her shoe toss, and the memory of me as a waiter.

We regained our composure. The break was good, something we both needed and using that time, we removed the banjo from its case and checked it closely…we could see nothing but the maker's name, printed on a nice label and glued to the inside the body.

CHAPTER 26

Gertrude continued to deride Ruth and Nathaniel telling them she didn't care how much they could have made, she was sick and tired of the stupidity, always caused by them, that plagued the family.

Nathaniel and Ruth were reaching a point of no return. It was she that disposed of the instruments, they were coerced into being accomplices to her schemes. She was the one who mistreated them, not the other way around. She was the one who could not say a good word about anyone, and that included them. Shamefully, she taught them the rules of snobbism and self-absorption. They weren't proud of it, but practiced it in an effort to please their mother.

Finally, Nathaniel courageously told her, that enough was enough. That he and Ruth had tried to please her in every way. Because of her they had lost what few friends they ever had. He pointed out that if they were to continue in the ways she taught them, all they'd ever have was money, and money wouldn't bring happiness!

She retaliated that he was a wimp, and that probably he would have gone through his father's money like water, if it hadn't been for her. Then, facing Ruth, she said that neither of them appreciated what she had done for the family! Money was most important!

Ruth, trying very hard to think positive thoughts, answered her saying that they did appreciate what she tried to do for them but they both realized that they had become bitter and wicked. She continued telling her that what few people tolerated them, were disgusted with them. Ruth continued accusing her of browbeating their father so that he spent most of his time with that group he jammed with, then taking it step further, suggested their father didn't want to come home, and when he did, he went into his study and closed the door.

Gertrude's face became contorted to the point she could have easily passed for one of the witches in "The Wizard of Oz." She shouted that she didn't know how they could say these things to her after all that she had done for them.

Nathaniel answered, "Yeah, 'all you had done for them,' like making father redo this home to have four rooms off of the living room, so we could be separated with individual cells to live in." Then he asked how often did they have a family dinner, or a night out? Gertrude responded it was her thought that those silly things cost money, and said that a night out more than once a year was a ridiculous waste.

Ruth, tears in her eyes, screamed that she wasn't going to stay there any longer. She had the money father left her, in her account, and she was going to start over somewhere where there were normal, pleasant, and nice people! She turned her heel, and with tears in her eyes, left the room and slammed the door behind her.

Nathaniel told his mother that he couldn't blame his sister, agreeing that there was no respect, no love, or anything else that other families have, and he continued telling her that even the people who came to their dinner party were happy to leave as quickly as possible, after her foolish request about the instruments.

Gertrude's demeanor softened. She bit her tongue when she asked that he not speak to her like that. The contortions of her mouth, the furrows in her forehead, even the hatred in her eyes seemed to fade as she made her final plea, requesting that he should have known, that all the things she did was to show that she only had done them for him and his sister.

He responded that they didn't believe that, and that she had eliminated all of the reasons that families stay together. When father was there, even browbeaten, and frequently cowed by her, he still could smile, and even make a joke from time to time!

Gertrude had been put in her place. She began to realize that there was more to life than money and possessions. In confronting her own persona, tears actually came into her eyes. She sat down on the sofa behind her, with her head in her hands, and sobs could be heard throughout the house.

He told her he was sorry, but since sis was

leaving that den of iniquity, he thought it was time for him to leave as well. As Nathaniel started toward the front door, the doorbell rang. He answered the door to discover a tall gentleman standing on the porch. The tall gentleman looked down at him and asked if he was John's son.

Gertrude started to stand, and with tears still streaming down her face, she pulled a handkerchief from here wrist band and tried to wipe them away. Then she realized who was at the door. Shocked, she called his name and asked what on earth he was doing there.

Nathaniel turned to his mother and questioned, do you know this man? Her expression changed and she told him it wasn't important, they would talk about it later.

Without a flinch, a smile, or a frown, Frank walked into the room past the surprised Nathaniel, and confronted the sister-in-law he had not seen for over 23 years. He confronted her saying it seemed to him she should at least let the young man know who he was, since he didn't seem to even rate a hello, or a "how have you been," or a "do you need anything?"

She raised her voice and asked Frank what he wanted, and before he could answer, she added that he didn't even have the decency to come to his brother's funeral. He maintained control of himself, answering he didn't know John was gone because she didn't let him know; he then addressed her as "you old leech."

Not to be intimidated Gertrude answered he best not start with her because she was in no mood to put up with him. Then she told him to just tell her what he wanted and get it over with, accusing him that the reason he was there was because he wanted something!

Frank turned to face Nathaniel and told him who he was, and that he assumed he never knew he had an uncle. Nathaniel responded that he didn't, because no one ever mentioned Barry having a father, then he asked Frank where he had been. Frank gave him a short answer of, "Let's just say I've been away. Okay?"

Turning to face Gertrude, he told her if that was the way she wanted it, well and good, just give him his banjo, the one John liked to play. He reminded her that it was his, and John was only keeping it for him. Gertrude' face turned a pale shade of gray. So many years had passed since she saw to it he went to prison for embezzlement, that she had forgotten how John had obtained that banjo. Knowing she was wrong, she said she didn't remember that. Frank finally lost his temper and told her to quit messing with him, he called her Gertie, and continued telling her he was in no mood for her lies. He further told her that she may have bullied John all those years, but he suggested she should not try it with him.

Gertrude cut him off and shouted that was enough, that she didn't have the banjo and had no idea where it was, then she made the mistake of telling him to get out! He reached out and grabbed her. Nathaniel, without thinking it through very well, leaped onto his uncle's back in an effort to relieve the pressure Frank was exerting on his mother's shoulder. It was like a fly on a horse. Frank moved his right arm behind his neck, and extending his hand he grasped the back of his nephew's neck. He leaned his large body to the side and threw Nathaniel to the floor without loosening the grasp he had on Gertrude's shoulder.

Nathaniel lay in a heap on the floor. His breath was labored, but he was unhurt. Frank squeezed harder on Gertrude's shoulder and threatened that he was only going to ask her one more time where his banjo was, and he wanted the truth.

Nathaniel struggled to a sitting position, his legs twisted, like they might have been if he was shooting craps. He wondered what happened, but new better than to say anything for fear Frank would tear his mother's shoulder completely off. He waited to hear his mother's explanation.

Gertrude winced with pain, but Frank pressed harder. He told her she could be hurt worse, and would be, if she didn't give him the answer that he requested. She realized her predicament and suggested that if he would let go, she would tell him what he wanted to know. Frank, knowing her well, answered that she should tell him first, and then he would let her loose.

She agreed and he relaxed his grip a little, but did not totally release her. She told him about the instruments, and that they were just in the way. She wanted to redo John's den, but to accomplish that, she had to get rid of his things, including both instruments. She told him she sold them to Ben, down at the antique shop.

He repeated, "Sold to Ben?" and asked what she was thinking. He shouted that he had spent $2,000.00 on the banjo when he bought it 28 years ago. Then he asked again, what was she thinking, selling it to an antique dealer? Shaking his head in disbelief, he asked what she got for it. She told him she received $100.00 and thought it was a bargain because she hated that thing from the first day he bought it! She tried to tell him that after thinking about it, she attempted to buy it back. He didn't believe her!

He told her he could not understand why John tolerated her all of those years and what a miserable excuse for a woman she was.

Having recovered from his thrashing, he told his uncle that was enough, and he tried to look as tough as he could while threatening him with, if he didn't let go of his mother...then Nathaniel started to get up. Frank admired his courage but grabbing his shoulder, suggested it would be wise for Nathaniel to stay where he was.

Nathaniel, now with his own shoulder in pain, nodded that he understood, then Frank, turning his attention back to his sister-in-law, and thinking about what she said earlier, asked why she would want it back if she hated it so.

Now Gertrude was in a bad place. He had her in his clinches, and wasn't going to accept anything except the truth, so under duress she told him that some woman wanted to buy it for a company out East, and they told her that they would have to discuss selling it. She continued about their visit with Ben and the offer of $100.00 they made, but that he wouldn't budge. She continued telling him how they went from the $100.00 he gave them, up to $400.00, and that was when he told them that he had sold it to someone else.

Frank was then even more irritated with her story and told her she was an idiot, and much too stupid to consider that just by his being in the antique business, he would have a pretty good idea about how much it was worth. He released his grip on her shoulder and let her sit down on the sofa. By now, Nathaniel, keeping his distance from his uncle, crept to an overstuffed chair that set between his door and his sister's door.

Gertrude told him that the instruments were gone, probably forever, and asked why they were so important to him. He answered her that was his concern, and she would never understand anything like 'sentimental value.' Gertrude was frightened and blurted out that maybe Frank's son had them both.

He angrily answered, what did she mean, [his] son? She stole him from him too! He hadn't forgotten what she did to him. He was sure that Mary might have forgiven her, but he wouldn't.

Frank was boiling! He didn't move or blink an eye. His memory was very vivid. He remembered how his brother, knowing Frank was innocent, tried to raise his son. He remembered all of those letters he wrote coming back unopened. He remembered how his wife died in a strange accident... one that was never solved. He remembered how his brother John, tried to get the insurance money issued to him, but failed when the court awarded the money to Barry, and to be handled as a trust by Gertrude, until his 18st birthday. He remembered a lot more than his sister-in-law would have liked.

Badgered by Frank, Gertrude accused him of living with a woman without wedlock in an effort to embarrass him. It didn't work, and he informed her that he and Madge were legally married, several months after he moved to Willowpoint, Alabama.

Madge! How could he have forgotten that he left her in his blue sedan? She could have been listening to everything being discussed. He knew she'd go after that banjo in a minute if it meant a buck or two was to be had, and he was also was well aware of the havoc she could cause. He dashed out of the house to check on her, leaving a threat of violence if the family lied to him as he rushed out. Before he had taken ten steps, he realized that he had no address for his son. He turned around and re-entered, without knocking! Nathaniel was still in his chair, staring at his mother. In a demanding voice, he demanded they give him Barry's address. Both Nathaniel and Gertrude looked at him with fear. His brazen approach before was bad enough, but coming into their home a second time, unannounced, was far more frightening!

Gertrude, still frightened, but with her deceitful attitude still intact, told him that she had no idea where to find Barry and again told him to get out of her house! Not liking to be threatened by her, he got in her face and told her he was only asking this... one last time.

Nathaniel put his hand in front of his face, for protection, and told his uncle that she didn't know the address, and pleaded with his uncle to not hurt them. Frank looked down at him and told him to get his hand out from in front of his face and be a man! If he knew where the address was...Nathaniel ran into his room and got the information. Returning, he gave his uncle the address, and pleaded with Frank to leave them alone. Frank, sickened by the two of them, turned and left.

Gertrude questioned the wisdom of giving the address to her brother-in-law. Nathaniel, with an insidious smile, answered why not, they didn't care for Barry anyway; he thought that the two of them would have a very interesting meeting. Gertrude smiled in agreement with his action.

Frank, discovered Madge had not moved, but was asleep in the front seat where he had left her. With Barry's address in hand, he pulled a city map from the glove box, studied it for a few minutes, then drew a circle around 4004 Willow Drive, Guntersville.

Pulling up in front of the place, he checked his hair, and looked into the rearview mirror and checked his teeth to be sure there wasn't any leftover food stuck between them. He wanted to look as well as he could, meeting his adult son for the first time.

Barry had just come out of his apartment and started down the walk when Frank, not knowing it was his son, stopped him to ask if he knew if Barry Dono was at home. Barry, still very much worried about his own safety since his friend's murder, asked why he wanted to know.

Frank told him that he hadn't seen Barry in a while, and thought, since he was told that he lived there, he might know if his son was home or not. Barry was shocked. He wasn't aware his dad was anywhere close by. He didn't remember ever seeing him, not even a picture. Uncle John rarely mentioned him, except to say that he was gone!

Frank took a step back, then took a closer look at him and asked if he was Barry. Barry, still concerned about the two recent murders, asked how he knew he had the right address. Frank told him he had eyes like his mother had, and the same features, then grimaced before adding a brief ending of, "Under all of that garbage on your face." Barry countered by asking why, if he was Barry's dad, did he show up now. Then he asked Frank to show him some identification.

Frank laughed and told him he had to be Barry all right, asking for identification. Then he smiled and asked if his mother was Mary Joseph. Taken by surprise, he stuttered an answer that he guessed so, and consequently, Frank was indeed his father. He told Barry that when he was a kid, he stuttered too. A speech therapist in college helped him overcome it.

Then he told him there was no doubt that he was his father.

Barry had to consider that this big fellow could actually be his dad. He asked where he had been and where had he come from? Then, remembering all the lies that his aunt had told him, he asked what his father wanted. Frank answered with a question of his own, asking if that was what all the people in town wanted to ask was, what did he want? He asked if it really was too much that he might want to see his family, after all of those years. Thinking for a minute, Barry considered that it was reasonable to ask, but he wondered what else people could consider.

Frank told him that he came back to get his banjo because John told him a long time ago that when he came home, be sure and find it, because it was his and it had a very special value.

Barry was at a loss. He told his father that he didn't know what he was talking about, and that before Uncle John died, he told him that he could have it. Frank became incensed, and told his son that he had come at the right time. He said that John was keeping it for him, but if he gave it to Barry, he must have assumed that he would never come back for it, consequently, the safest place for it to be kept would be with his son. Maybe John believed that he would be gone forever and that Barry should have whatever it was to have.

Barry, not knowing much about his father, asked

if he played the instrument. Frank answered that he was, at one time, a very good banjo picker. Thinking they had a lot to talk about, Frank asked him if they could go someplace close by for a cup of coffee. Barry agreed it was good idea and suggested Joe's place, as it was close by. He climbed into Frank's blue sedan, and discovered a woman sleeping in the back seat. He asked if that was his father's wife, and Frank said, yes, for now.

CHAPTER 27

Frank saw Joe behind the serving window and asked for three cups of coffee by pointing three fingers at the booth.

Madge, still blurry eyed from sleeping, sat like a zombie, and after staring around the café, she disgustedly blurted out to her husband, that she thought they was goin' to someplace nice. Of course Joe heard her and told her if she didn't like it there, she could always go someplace else. Frank stared at Madge, embarrassed, he told her to settle down, after all his son had to live here. Frank introduced the woman to his son, as his wife, Madge. There were a lot of questions asked and answered between Barry and Frank. During their discourse, Frank mentioned his call on the Gertrude Dono household. Barry, in turn, told him about her dinner party and her request to the guests for information about the instruments. Frank, hearing that, realized that Gertrude really didn't know where the banjo was and probably for the first time might be telling the truth.

The discussion brought to light a lot of questions Barry had about the reason for Frank's disappearance, the loss of his first wife and Barry's mother, as well as what happened to Barry, and why his father was not able to be there for him.

I had an appetite for a cup of Joe's coffee, rather than my own so I wandered down around the corner. I was surprised to walk into Joe's place and see Barry sitting with Frank and Madge. He looked uncomfortable, so I stopped at the booth where they were sitting, and made some small talk about not having seen Barry for some time, and we were wondering if he was okay. Lori and I missed him.

Looking relieved, Barry answered that it had been a few weeks since we had seen each other and asked me to sit down with them. Frank suggested that the conversation was personal, but. Barry insisted it was okay because I was in his employ and could hear anything being talked about. You could cut the tension with a knife and I could feel it growing. Frank seemed like a reasonable man when Lori and I were with him earlier so it made me wonder if Madge might be the reason for his comments about the two having a private conversation.

Frank looked up at me, and his eyes told me he was playing a game... I still had the feeling Madge had something to do with his change so I took the queue from Frank, and suggested that when they were finished with their coffee, Barry should stop by and see Lori and me. Frank suggested that if it was important, perhaps Barry could stop by the office while he and Madge finished their coffee.

We left Joe's place and walked the short distance to our office. Lori met us there as though we had arranged in advance to meet at that time, which we did not. I explained that Barry and I met at the greasy spoon where he was having a conversation with his father and Madge. I was about to ask Barry about his meeting with them, when Lori reached into her purse, and turned on her recorder without removing it. I was glad she carried one, just for extreme emergencies…and this was one!

Barry floored me when he spoke with such few hesitations like he usually had. He told us that before hiring us, he did some research himself. It was then that he discovered his father was not only still alive, but that he had remarried, after getting out of prison, to a Madge O'Hara. In doing research on her, he found she had a brother, Sean. To Barry's chagrin, he found Sean was living here, but supposedly didn't know his sister, Madge lived in Willow Point, since they had not communicated in years.

This piqued my curiosity so I asked if he had any further dealings with Sean to which he responded that they would meet occasionally in Huntsville, at a karaoke club, where they'd do a couple of songs, have a beer, or two, and that was about it. It appeared to Barry that he had made a new acquaintance, and hopefully he could get more knowledge about his estranged family.

Could Sean have contacted Madge, during their conversation and learned about his new friend, Barry and put two and two together figuring there was in inheritance or something?

I snapped back to reality and asked Barry if Sean might have mentioned anything about his relationship with Madge. Barry stared at the floor contemplating an answer. He raised his eyes to meet mine and told us that he didn't recall asking anything about any relationship, or about his family either, but he remember mentioning the instruments.

I eased into the fact that Sean had been murdered. Barry almost went into shock that his new friend has been killed! He stared at me in disbelief and repeated the word "killed" a couple of times in hearing about the loss of his new friend.

I explained that I was assisting a detective friend of mine and went to help him handle another investigation, and when we got to the address, we found Sean laying inside, on the floor.

He took a deep breath and uttered the word "Killed" again.

I asked if he had read about the murder of a girl named Mary Joseph, and he answered that he had, and wondered why I was asking the question. We were both a bit skeptical that he didn't show more emotion hearing her name, so Lori questioned why he didn't know that Mary Joseph was his half-sister. Barry looked at us in complete astonishment. It was clear that although he had done some research, the information that his father had another child, a girl, his half-sister?

His complexion whitened. He looked like he had seen a ghost, but maintained his composure as he asked if there was anything else he should know. We told him, as far as we knew, that was all we knew. Then I asked him if there was anything else he had to tell us. He said there was not, and that he felt guilty about not divulging his knowledge, what there was of it, about Sean.

Being Barry, he arose from his chair, and saying nothing, with slumped shoulders, he left.

CHAPTER 28

After Barry left, I asked Lori if she thought felt that Barry told us everything. She appeared to be irritated at me, and stated her opinion that he came to us in good faith, and we owed him our trust and should continue with our efforts to locate those instruments, regardless of the murders and the new light on the case.

I wasn't sure that the murders had anything to do with our case. Maybe it was Will's collection efforts that were the real problem. It was Sean, his client, that was murdered, and it was Sean's apartment where we found Mary. The things that connected this with our client, were the fact that his father, Frank was Sean's brother-in-law, and Mary Joseph was his half-sister. We had to assume that Barry had nothing to do with any of this; he was just the unlucky guy most folks would be pointing a finger at.

I questioned that, if none of this related to our client, then why did Frank and Mary Joseph suddenly show up out of nowhere. It seemed that everything started happening after we saw Sean and Barry together, then later we discover that Sean was murdered.

Lori started with that left foot scratching the top of her right one. Silence took over our conversation as she tried to come up with an answer. After mulling it over, she arrived at the possible conclusion that with his need for family, he may have discovered Sean was a shirttail relative and sought him out. While in an intoxicated condition, he told Sean about his Uncle John, the valuable instruments, and how they seemed to disappear after his uncle's death. It probably was their first meeting, instead of what I had been suggesting.

I drifted off into thought, trying to piece together, her thoughts and my own, when she shocked me out of my thoughts by asking if I was following her thoughts so far. I told her that I did. She continued how she thought Sean may have contacted his older sister, Madge. He probably thought there might be something of value to be had and agreed that they should try to find Mary Joseph. Since the apple doesn't fall far from the tree, as they say, Sean was Madge's brother and they may have been in more contact than we were aware of.

Her theory made a lot of sense, so we decided to visit Frank and Madge again, but I told Lori that first, I needed to stop at the bank.

I couldn't help but admire the old building every time I saw it. It was beautifully landscaped and located in the center of town. There were two pillars in the front, one needing a bit of repair, the other looking like the day they put it in place. The two automatic doors opened for us to enter the marble-floored lobby. This was not just any bank, it was my bank!

Lori asked if I was going to get some cash or something, and I told her no, I was not. Instead I told her that we were going to talk to Jack Falcone. We entered the small lobby on the right side of the bank and a young receptionist asked if she could help us. I told her she could, if she would advise Mr. Falcone that we would like to see him. She asked my name, and I told her it was Bill Deavereau.

As she walked away, Lori asked me why we wanted to talk to Jack Falcone, since she wasn't aware of any banking problems with the agency. I started to explain when Jack came out, extending his hand, and asking how he could help us. I suggested that we should talk in his office, as it was of a personal nature. We followed him the short distance from the reception area to his office, went in, and he closed the door.

He asked if we needed a loan, or something else the bank had to offer. I reminded him that a few days before I had called him about a client of ours, a Mr. Sean O'Hara. He indicated that he did remember that. I told him that Sean had mentioned that he (Mr. Falcone) was not only his immediate superior, but was also a kind of business consultant, after hours. He agreed that was true, but assured us that it was in no way to be inferred that had anything to do with regular bank business.

Falcone seemed deeply affected by Sean's death. He was very business-like and consoling with respect to the news. I told him that before Sean was murdered, he told us that he had asked him about how bearer bonds worked, in a general way, but apparently, he didn't understand the answer.

Jack answered that he did explain how they worked, and was surprised to learn that he didn't understand the explanation. I told him I understood that sometimes we just don't do well in explaining things and the person we are explaining to, was too embarrassed to ask twice. Then I asked if he had mentioned the purchase of an old mandolin. He fidgeted in his chair and seemed a little nervous at my question and immediately told us that he didn't remember any discussion regarding an instrument.

Jack's face lost some of its color. He seemed to be searching for the right words, while drumming his fingers on the desktop. He stopped drumming and told us that after rethinking their conversations, he did seem to remember a brief conversation about an old instrument. Then he asked me why we were asking about that.

I told him that we were hoping he might recall something Barry may have said, because we had another client who was also looking for a mandolin… and a banjo. I continued my query that I thought maybe Sean's questioning about the value of his collection, might be of value to us.

Falcone told us he was sorry he could not be of more help to us, but he didn't know much about

Sean's dealings. He asked if there was anything else he might help us with, as he had another appointment.

Looking directly at him I asked, just so I was clear about it, do bearer bonds lose their value?

Jack fidgeted with the pencil on his desk. It was apparent that I had hit a nerve. He told me that anyone could cash a bearer bond, and since they were paid for in cash or the equivalent, they did not lose their value. I told him that was all I wanted to know. Lori and I stood, told him we knew how valuable his time was, thanked him, and left his office.

Originally, my plan was to wait outside of the bank to see if he would leave right away, but I changed my mind when Lori started asking questions. She asked what that meeting was all about. I told her to think about our meeting with Sean. She said she did recall the meeting but not that subject.

I smiled at her, and told her that I didn't think she ever forgot anything. Bewildered, she said that she couldn't remember anything about Sean saying he talked to Falcone about any instruments, if that was what he was referring to. I congratulated her, and told her that was because Sean [didn't] say anything about instruments!

Lori's face brightened when she put two and two together! She realized that if Sean didn't mention them to us, then how could Falcone know about them? The only way that could be, would be if Sean told him about it, because it was for sure Barry didn't, and no one else knew about them, except maybe for Madge, who we were not sure about yet. Regardless, that still meant at least the two of them were in on this together, and with Madge, somehow in the picture.

It was Lori's thought, a long time ago, that maybe something was hidden inside the instruments. One thing that would remain valuable and anyone could cash in, would be bearer bonds. I asked her if she noticed how nervous it made Jack when I asked about them. She said she did, and then asked me if I thought bonds could be hidden inside the instruments. I smiled and answered, that I had no idea, but I thought we should find out.

My next stop was Frank's place. I felt like I might be taking my life into my own hands so we stopped a little ways from his apartment, to watch the coming and going. We hoped that being early in the day, it wouldn't be a waste of time. Several minutes passed before we saw a new Ford Mustang Convertible pull up in front of the place. It was Jack Falcone! I wish I could have said it was a surprise, but it wasn't!

We waited until Jack came out, got into his Mustang, and drove off. I thought about following him, but decided maybe Frank might be coming out...I was wrong! It was Madge who came out and walked down the street to their vehicle, got in and left.

As soon as she was out of sight, I, used the burglar tool I always carry and picked the lock in the front door. There were many ideal places to hide a remote listening device. The apartment had several holes in the walls to hide my listening device in. I removed it from my pocket and placed it in a small hole, close to the ceiling. While I was there, I looked around the place but found little of value, except for one thing…a picture of a person I recognized, but didn't remember seeing there on my last visit. Mary Joseph!

I locked the door and returned to the car where Lori, who was impatiently sitting in the front seat, asked me if I learned anything new. I told her about the picture, but that was all that was new, except for the surveillance device I left hidden high in the wall.

CHAPTER 29

With all of the new information about the family, and knowing that Gertrude was concerned her brother-in-law had returned and wanted the banjo, there had to be more to the story. Following her original deception, Lori decided to continue her investigation, She drove to their residence thinking surveillance might turn up something, and waited...she was right.

Gertrude and Nathaniel came out of the side door of the house and got into their car. After they pulled away Lori followed, maintaining a reasonable distance between them and her. A few blocks from the antique shop they stopped and got out. Lori keeping a safe distance, pulled to the curb behind a pick-up truck. She watched as they stood on the sidewalk, taking a close look each direction, checking to be sure no one was watching. Lori's suspicions were rewarded when she saw them enter the home they parked in front of and the person who opened the door, also checked up and down the street before closing the door.

Getting out of her car, she carefully made her way to the side of the house. There were several large bushes there, and one was near to a large window. She moved as close to the window as possible with the stealth of a cat.

She could hear Gertrude telling the occupant

that she and Nathaniel knew that he knew where the mandolin was. She told him they wanted it. He answered, that they had come to the wrong place because he had no idea what they were talking about!

Gertrude answered him with her loud and agitating voice, called him a liar, and that he had been with that bunch of old bats for years, and she knew that he knew a lot more than he was letting on. She said that John had talked about him, and they knew more than he thought they did.

Loudly, he answered, that he doubted John ever talked about the group because they were all friends, not gossips like her.

She shouted that they were going to watch him very closely because they needed that instrument. Then she started to threaten him, but he stopped her short, telling her that he wouldn't tell them anything even if he did know where it was, which he didn't! He also told her that she was the most aggravating person in the world and wondered how John tolerated her. Finally, as a last resort, he told them to get out of his house before he called the police, and ushered them to the front door, practically shoving them out, with mother and son grumbling all the while.

Lori stayed in her hiding place, waiting for them to get into their car and leave. Not paying attention to her surroundings, she was suddenly jolted to reality when a hand grabbed her by the shoulder. He told her that he didn't know who she was, but she had better come out of those bushes! How he knew she was there was baffling, but know, he did.

He asked her to tell him why she was there. She alluded to the fact that she had been listening at the window. He told her that she was kind of young and pretty to be a [peeping tom] type, and suggested that she not lie to him because he didn't like liars.

Lori tried to pull away, but he held her arm tightly. He was too strong for her to break his hold on her. Frightened, she explained she was following his recent visitors, and that he couldn't dislike them than any more than she did, explaining that they tried to kidnap her a few days ago and thought that they wanted to kill her. He stood back and looked her, then he informed her that following them to his place wasn't something she should have done. She responded that she knew that now, and she was sorry for appearing to be a 'peeping tom.' He let her go, but admonished her action and suggested that she not let him see her there again!

Lori was embarrassed to be caught, but happy to be released. At least this time she wasn't hurt, just let go with a strong message. She got into her car and made a note of the address. She was curious who this man could be. After arriving back at the office she started a search on her computer for the owner of that address. She was astounded to discover that he was Guy Billings, one of the players from John's group. Now even more determined to discover why the Dono family had called on him, and not the others in the group, Lori poured over her notes to see if something that they had written might shed some light on the situation. Turning her attention to the white board, she was shocked to feel the presence of someone else in the room. The hair stood up on the back of her neck as she turned to face the intruder.

He asked if she was Lori. She said she was. Finding out that he was right, he told her to be calm, he wasn't there to harm her. She regained her composure and asked what he wanted.

Surprised she didn't recognize him, since they met earlier at his place, he told her he was Frank Dono, and he was there to return something that Deavereau had left in his place. She asked him what it was and he handed her the listening device. He told her he found it, and to tell Deavereau that they had something in common. Without saying another word, he turned and left as quietly as he had come into the office.

Still jittery after being scared out of her wits, Lori called me and explained what had just happened. I wasn't too pleased with myself regarding the apparent poor placement of the listening device in Frank's place, but I was curious that he said we had something in common. I had to find out what it was.

I drove to his place, mulling over what I might discover when I got there, and wondered what we supposedly had in common. I knocked on his door, and a cold chill went up my spine. I wondered if I was walking into a trap. Madge opened the door and asked me what I wanted. I told her Frank had been to my office and left a calling card.

He was there and told Madge to let me him. I entered and immediately asked him what we had in common. Without answering, he got up from his chair, shook my hand, and asked me to have a seat. Confused and concerned, I took the chair across from him.

He told Madge to go shopping, then he paused until she closed the door behind her. When he was sure she was gone he told me why he asked for this meeting. Leaning forward in his chair, with his face so close to mine I could feel his breath, as he told me, this was the deal, they had come to get his banjo. He didn't know about all of the hoop-la concerning the thing. He said that a week or so ago, Sean called his sister and told her that my brother had passed away. He didn't think anything about it because he knew that Madge and Sean did speak occasionally on the phone. What he didn't know, until now, was that his daughter was living in Guntersville too.

His face remained a blank page as he spoke. It was difficult to read his true feelings, as they were hidden behind a wall of nothingness. I wanted to ask him a lot of questions, but I knew that if I remained silent, he was going to tell me what I needed to know.

He told me the reasons for his leaving, and not returning. Apparently, years ago, his brother told him that when he (John) was gone, there would be something for him, all he had to do was come back and pick up the banjo, and all would be revealed. Then he continued, telling me that he went to see his sister-in-law, but she wouldn't tell him where it was. Instead, she told him that she sold it to someone, she went to purchase it back, and that person wouldn't sell it back to her because, he had sold it, and told her that was that!

I told him that I found out that same information and that we were also searching for that banjo, and his brother's mandolin, because we were hired to find them by his son. I told Frank that Barry had given us very well documented info on the mandolin, and descriptive stuff on the banjo, stating that the fact it had the pearl inlaid Indian headdress engraved and painted on it made it priceless. I told him, in confidence, that we had found the banjo and had not told Barry yet.

I asked him where he had been all of this time. I thought, for his son's sake it was time to come clean

Frank told me what he knew, how he had kept a watch on his sister-in-law's place at the same time that Lori appeared on the scene. He figured that she must have known something about the banjo that he didn't. He had assumed that she and the family were in cahoots to get his banjo, and he didn't know why. When Lori and I showed up at his place earlier, he realized who she was and decided to talk to me, face to face, when it seemed convenient. My planting of the device, made the time right for our discussion and the lost instruments were what we had in common.

I explained that when he and Madge entered the picture, we knew who they were, but not why they were here, and since their arrival, two people had been murdered. He could see why they remained pretty high on the suspect list. I told him that if he knew anything he thought that I should know, this would be the time. We weren't concerned with family problems, only finding what Barry was paying us to locate.

Looking at my watch, I told Frank I had to leave and suggested that we get together again soon to compare the rest of our notes. He agreed. As I turned to leave, I noticed a new package of banjo strings laying on the table and felt his need to find the instrument.

The suspect list was dwindling. We needed to take a closer look at Madge. When I returned to the office I stepped into Lori's office and filled her in on what I found out from Frank. I told her I thought Sean called on the phone, and sent a note to his sister, Madge. Frank supposedly got it by mistake! The information in the note was really about both of the instruments, even though it appeared to be a simple suggestion to come to Guntersville to get his banjo. He, (Sean) probably had called and told Madge that he had met this guitar player named Barry, and after a drink or two, he mentioned that his father was Frank Dono. He also told her that Barry was searching for a banjo and described it, so she, being aware of the story Frank mentioned, concocted the idea of a note mysteriously sent to her, but to be mistakenly received by Frank.

Lori asked why they didn't come and talk to Barry instead of being so secretive. I answered that they probably came to do just that, but she discovered there was a lot more to the story, after talking to Sean before he was murdered. Frank, not having seen Barry for years, had no idea what he had been told so he felt it was necessary to play it cool for a while. It was then that Barry must have mentioned to his new friend, Sean, that the mandolin was worth a considerable amount of money. To further that chain of thought, the uncle, John, in his last few words to Barry, suggested the same thing that Frank told us, that "the banjo would reveal the true value."

Lori answered that I had two conversations with Frank; one when she was there, and one when she wasn't. At the first one I asked many questions and so did she. The second time, he asked that only I should come. She asked why he did that. I had no answer. I told her that was how I found out that Sean had contacted his mother, before he was killed. We both had an immediate reaction, and our thoughts collided. "Contacted his sister before he was killed" It was as though our minds came together, like a mind meld from Star Trek.

Lori remembered Barry telling Sean about the instruments. Sean knew his older sister and her husband were coming to town. Barry might have known that John had left something for his father, probably inside of the banjo.

We decided that we should take another look inside of it since it was in our storage area. Rushing to the closet, we removed the banjo case, and placed a small observation lens into the sound hole. Moving it around like you would if you placed it under a door, we were able to see a tiny envelope inside, glued to the top next to the sound hole.

> *The question now was, should we take it out, or should we not? What had Uncle John left his brother? Was it a code that only the two of them understood?*

We ventured a guess that it could be a microdot inside the tiny envelope. At that time of the twentieth century, they were being used a lot.

CHAPER 30

Madge wasn't pleased when she found out that Frank called a meeting with me. She felt that the meeting left her vulnerable to scrutiny. Frank, on the other hand, felt he had made headway with me, not fully realizing that his wife might be the answer to most of the questions we all had. With her gutter language, she told Frank that she didn't see why it was necessary to talk to me. She told him that I wasn't carin' about them much, and that all I wanted to do was to find out where that banjo was.

Frank didn't like her attitude and bluntly told her that just because she had no feelings for the instrument, didn't mean that he shouldn't. He let her know that he was an educated person, he didn't talk like her, and that she should wise up and talk more intelligently! Not to be intimidated, Madge suggested that just because he was educated, didn't mean he was better than she was.

Frank reached behind his chair, and picking up the banjo strings he had recently purchased, he told her that he just bought them so when he got the banjo back, he could put new strings on it and revive old memories, like those old times with his brother, John.

Madge continued her tirade, shouting that he ain't bin aplayin' since she knowed him, and that's been some time. Their disagreement lasted over an hour until Frank finally tired of it and suggested that they, putting their differences aside, should concentrate on the fact that it was strange that their daughter and her brother had both been murdered.

She agreed, and stated that maybe they could be next. Frank answered that he thought that way too, but he couldn't help wonder why those particular people were murdered, and he was concerned that the note he received might have had something to do with the murders. Madge, not revealing that the note was really to her, replied that she couldn't believe that, and asked, "Who woulda knowed about it anyhow?"

He told Madge that he never knew that the two of them actually knew each other. He had never met Sean, and to his knowledge, Sean never met Mary, so he questioned what the connection could be. Frank put the banjo strings back on the table and paced around the room deep in thought, with his thumb beside his mouth, and his fingers clamped lightly around his chin, as though stroking a goatee. He wondered since Sean had a friend, like Barry, if he could have mentioned something about the instruments and their value.

Frank told her he thought that they should talk to Barry again. He felt that there was something going on, and Barry might have the answer. Madge followed Frank to the door and watched as he drove off.

CHAPTER 31

It was a strenuous day for Barry, everything went wrong. We didn't turn up anything new about the mandolin, and we didn't tell him the good news about the banjo. His new acquaintance was dead, and the gigs weren't coming fast enough to meet his everyday expenses. He even considered that he should not have been so eager to agree to the terms of the investigation.

Having no one else to discuss things with, he called his cousin, Nathaniel. Although there was no love lost between them, Nathaniel had extended his hand in friendship offering the invitation to dinner. Barry thought that maybe it was true that the Dono family could become a unit once again, after these many years. After all, he knew that his father, Frank, was no longer a young man and his Aunt Gertrude was getting up in years as well.

He called Nathaniel on the phone and invited him to a concert. Nathaniel played it cool, being suspicious of everyone and everything, in accordance with his mother's teaching. He was brought up to trust no one, and he believed that anyone who befriended him had to be after his money. He told Barry that he didn't know if he could make it or not but needed to know what date and time. Barry told him that would depend on the type of music he liked, since there were a lot of concerts. Nathaniel answered that he liked the Blues. Excitedly, Barry told him he was in luck, because the Darby Trio would be in Huntsville that weekend.

Nathaniel was eager to say yes since his whole life had always been organized by his domineering mother. Still under her influence, he was compelled to tell his mother where he was going. Needing time to tell her, he asked for Barry's number and told him he would get back to him as soon as he was certain of his schedule. Barry had little choice but to agree, and told him that his number was 348-5551.

With the invitation extended, the [wait to see] if it would be accepted was in play. For Barry, this was a step forward in getting better acquainted with his cousin. They were about the same age, but that was where their identities ended. Barry's whole life was music. Nathaniel's whole life had been money management. The two didn't sound like a pairing made in Heaven.

Barry sat idly by, waiting to hear from his cousin. He thought about the instruments, he pondered about Guy, Billy Joe, and Tony, wondering if they were as good of friends to his uncle as everyone assumed they were. He considered a call to one of them hoping for an invitation to sit in on one of their practice sessions.

Sometimes you can learn a lot by just being in the right place at the right time and with the right people.

He decided to call Tony. When Tony answered he told him who it was and asked if he remembered him or not. Tony told him he certainly did and that the guys had just been talkin' about him during their jam session. Barry asked him if he could sit in with them once in a while, considering that he played several instruments, including the mandolin. Tony was delighted and told him they would love to have him and told him how his uncle had kept them [pretty much] up to date on his achievements. Tony told Barry that he was probably a lot better than they were, but with him 'sittin' in, they might just learn a thing or two.

Tony collecting his thoughts, told Barry that the next day would be just fine, that is, if he was free. Barry jumped at the opportunity, and accepted the invitation.

CHAPTER 32

I decided to call Detective Johnson again, so I punched in the number on the cell and in seconds Rob Johnson answered. I told him who was calling and he told me I was like a bad penny. I responded with, "Go ahead, belittle me, I was used to being intimidated by you cops."

After laughing at our comments, we decided to get down to business. I advised him that I planned to tell him a couple of things he probably didn't know, in the hopes that we could agree on helping each other. Sergeant Rob Johnson agreed, so I explained that we were looking for a banjo and a mandolin. He threw me a sarcastic "such a big deal, a banjo, and a mandolin." I told him a lot of what had been going on, but when I got to the part about who was in town, and why they were there, it seemed to peak his interest.

He asked how long I had been in contact with both Frank and Madge Dono. I told him a few days and added that they were a strange group, those Donos. I found out that he had an outstanding warrant for Frank's son, Barry and Rob asked what I knew about him. I wasn't going to just give out information, so I asked him what the warrant was for. He told me that he could not answer that question, so I told him that if he wasn't interested in the murders or what we knew about the Frank Dono family....

Understanding that I wasn't going to continue our conversation without more info from him, he tried for my sympathy with the old buddy crap about after all, he had rules he had to live by and yadda, yadda, yadda.

I agreed that I knew about the rules, but then I inserted that he should know that I shouldn't give out confidential information either, so I guessed he'd have to learn what I already knew, the hard way.

He tried to intimidate me, saying that he knew my friend Will and I were still not off the hook, since we found both of the murder victims before they did, and that made us persons of interest to the department. I answered that if they had any reason to suspect us, we'd have known by then and suggested he could do better, that is, if he wanted our cooperation.

Finally he agreed and reluctantly told us that Barry had an assault charge issued against him for assaulting a business owner, a Mr. Appleby. Allegedly he attacked him yesterday without provocation. For some reason or other he thought Appleby was hiding a banjo he said belonged to him. Unfortunately for Dono, no banjo was found in the store inventory, according to the investigator's report.

He was on a roll and kept talking so we kept listening. He asked if we knew that Frank Dono, John's brother, and Barry's father, was back in town? He filled us in on the story that, several years ago John Dono, was a wealthy investment partner and his brother was his partner. John's wife, Gertrude, filed a complaint accusing her brother-in-law of embezzlement. It was a pretty thin case, but the jury bought Gertrude Dono's testimony that Frank had taken money while she was in charge of the accounting. He got convicted and sent to prison. He indicated that it was all there at City Hall in the court records.

I was surprised by that one! It made me wonder how much more I might find Gertrude involved in. I thanked Rob and told him I would escort Barry in, to satisfy the warrant. Other than that, I told him that we had met Frank and Madge and had nothing more than he already seemed to know, but I would keep in apprised.

Although she tried to hear what was being said, Lori could not catch it all. She asked, so I told her the gist of the conversation. She was especially interested in what he said about Gertrude being the accountant, at the time of the embezzlement.

We added the information we now had, including some questions to our board.

Lori headed it,

<u>FACTS:</u>

Barry had attacked Ben Appleby, proprietor of the Antique Store.

Frank Dono was sent to prison for embezzlement.

Gertrude Dono had been in charge of accounting at Dono Investments in early years.

Gertrude Dono was chief witness against Frank's embezzlement charge

Frank Dono's son, Barry befriended Sean, Madge's son.

Frank's daughter was Mary Joseph, and befriended by Sean. Both Sean and Mary were killed with puncture wounds to juggler.

Ben Appleton now part of the jam group.

We studied what we had written on the board for a few minutes and a couple of things came to light. We both saw the need for another meeting with Barry. The morning was flying by and we decided he should be getting up to start his day. We left the office, and as we got into my Olds, again she asked why I kept the old bag of bolts instead of getting something I could be proud of.

I didn't answer her. She didn't understand my feeling for my old car. I had her since she was new and she was my only companion off and on, depending on what I was working on.

One of these days, old lizzy and I were going to have to part ways, but it would be like losing an old friend! But the timing was my business!

    We pulled up in front of Barry's place, which was still under some construction, but well on its way to completion. I knocked on the door and he opened it. His attire of bathrobe and slippers, and a sleepy look validated our assumption about it being time for him to get up.

    I cheerfully wished him good morning and asked if the coffee was on. He answered "no" to the good morning, and "yes" to the coffee being on. After excusing himself, he left to put some clothes on, and suggested we could get a cup from the cupboard since the coffee was hot and fresh.

    Making my way to the counter I opened the cabinet to an array of mugs, probably from the many places he had played at. I noticed one from a familiar town, the place Frank had come from, Willow Point. I chose another one, and asked Lori if she would like a cup. She said she would not, at least not right then. After pouring the coffee into my cup I returned to the living room to sit with Lori. I whispered that I just saw a cup from Willow Point. I knew that they had a pub there, but I wondered if it had any music, or if it was just a pub and sandwich bar.

    Lori did her foot thing, this time while sitting down. After a few seconds, she questioned, why would Barry go somewhere with no music? Especially a little place like Willow Point.

Before I could answer her, Barry came out, partially dressed but presentable. He was pleased we found the coffee, and asked if it was drinkable, remembering that Lori continuously complained about my mud. I told him that I thought it was great, strong enough to be tasty, by not thick like the glue I made.

We all three chuckled about my comment, then Barry asked if our visit was business or pleasure. I told him that we hadn't heard from him for a couple of days were concerned, with all that had been going on. I lied, not wanting him to know what we had found out from Sargent Johnson, so I asked if he had found out anything new, with respect to the missing instruments.

Barry, with his 'so honest' look told us that he did not know any more than he did the last time that we had talked. I was trying to decide whether or not to blind-side him about his altercation with Ben, or just let it play out to see if he would fill us in.

Lori, starting to work with that foot, was having a difficult time staying quiet. I had no doubt that something was going to come out of that lovely mouth. She asked Barry if he thought that the antique store had anything to do with the banjo disappearance. Barry, taken by surprise, blurted out that he didn't think so, at least he didn't… Then he stopped mid-sentence.

I picked up on that, and asked 'at least he didn't what? He told us it was nothing, he was just rambling on.

Pushing, we told him it was okay to be honest, we had that relationship, per our agreement, that he could tell us anything. I asked him to tell us, what it was that Ben didn't do.

He relented and told me that he hated to say that he got mad, but Ben got belligerent and wouldn't tell him why his aunt Gertrude was seeing him.

I knew he was lying to us since the sergeant had already told us he was there to confront Ben about the banjo.

My next question was, was Ben seeing Mrs. Dono? I took a step further and told him that we understand that they were enemies.

Barry looked like a puppy caught with the family dinner on the floor, when he answered that he really didn't know, that he just assumed, since the dinner party, that they were friends. I understood how he would think that, so I suggested that since he was about to get dressed we should probably leave. Barry seemed relieved that we were leaving. He stood, and when we moved to the door, he thanked us for coming and told us it was always good to see us.

After we left Lori's opinion was that something stunk, and she thought we should pull down the road a bit to see if he left. I agreed with her, and backed the car behind some equipment that was still parked around the place, making it impossible to see us.

In fewer than ten minutes Barry came out, got

into his car, and left. We followed. He drove straight to his aunt's home. Not getting out of his car, he was greeted, to our surprise, by Nathaniel. They shook hands, and Nathaniel, dressed with a sport shirt and coat, and those new tight pants the younger guys like to wear these days, continued down the steps to Barry's car.

We followed them to see where they were going. They were headed for Huntsville! That was a turn of events we hadn't considered.

CHAPTER 33

Frank called me and asked if he could see the banjo, I agreed that he could. It was less than a half hour later that he showed up. He thanked me for letting me see the banjo saying it has been several years since he saw it, or even to touch it. Then he asked if it was alright for Madge to be there too. I could hardly say anything but yes so they followed me to my office where the storage closet was. Lori, not being in favor of this meeting, stayed in the reception area, but with the door to my office open. She had her weapon in readiness, just in case of a problem.

I removed the case from the closet and handed it to Frank. At first he held it at arm's length drinking in the old case's beauty as if it were gold. After several moments he looked at Madge and told her that was what he had been talking about. He told her he thought she probably figured it would be some old smelly thing. Then he asked her if she didn't think it was a thing of beauty.

Madge, not being much for the love type stuff, simply replied it was better lookin' than she thought it would be. Not to be let down by her comment, he laid it on my desk and opened it. There, in all of its splendor, was the magnificent banjo. With its vivid decoration it almost took his breath away. He removed it from the case, found a pick in the center box, and proceeded to pluck it, ever so carefully. Then he turned to Madge once again, and remarked, that maybe now she could understand why he bought the strings. Madge, not intimidated by the remark, just stared, with glaring eyes, at the man she was married to.

He attempted to tune it, only to discover that when he did, one string immediately broke. He said it was time to put those new strings on it. He turned to me and said that he would like ask me one question, if that would be okay. I told him to ask away. It was that if I had searched the inside of the banjo for anything. I told him that we had, and he asked what we found. I, in turn, asked him what he expected us to find.

He replied that he didn't know. All he knew was what John told him what he told me; the real value was in the banjo. He told him that, the day Gertrude took it from him, and before he was sent to prison for the embezzlement charge.

I wanted to tell him, but Lori, who had been listening from the outer office, interrupted me. She stepped inside and told him that we did find something. It would not have been something that his brother would have put inside of it, at least not then because what we found wasn't available back then.

Madge spoke up calling Lori 'girlie' again, and

that they didn't need none of her yackin' right then and that she should let the boys do the talkin'.

Lori got that angry look and reminded her how she felt about that 'girlie' business. Before I could say anything, the two of them were inches apart. I grabbed Lori by the arms and Frank did the same with Madge. Frank told them both that was enough, and that Mr. Deavereau and he would complete the conversation...without both of them!

I spoke, as quietly as I could to Lori, telling her to go into the reception area and put on a pot of coffee. Angrily, she pulled away from me, and sullenly pouted as she marched out of my office, while Madge, also pouting, remained. Eventually she sat down in one of the office chairs.

Frank, quietly said he believed I had found something. I told him that we found a microdot, and that I had it in an envelope in my desk drawer. He asked to see it. I retrieved it and suggested it might be best if we both went together, to have it analyzed, and he agreed.

Immediately Madge told us that she thought the three of us should go. Of course, Lori, with her ear glued to the door, barged back into my office and said there would be bloodshed if she wasn't included. We felt it would be wise to take both cars, so Frank agreed to follow me.

He was reluctant to get out of his car when he discovered the place that I went to was the police station. I walked over and he opened the door window. He asked what we were doing there. I explained that Sergeant Johnson was a friend of ours. I also told him that the sergeant was totally aware of the age-old case against him and knew that he had served his time. Although he was still uneasy about going into the station, he finally realized he had nothing to be afraid of. Lori was inside before we were, her curiosity was ready to burst, while Madge, on the other hand, decided to stay in the car. That was no surprise to me, since I remembered that she had a warrant out for her arrest!

CHAPTER 34

A well-dressed gentleman came into the Alabama Credit Union, asking to speak to an executive of the branch. After a short wait, the vice-president, Mr. Egmont, invited him into his office and introduced himself. The gentleman, sank into the leather chair, across the desk from Mr. Egmont, and told him that his name was Jasper Grant, that he had recently moved here from Connecticut, and would like to open an account, and rent a security box.

Mr. Egmont asked him, as he did every new customer, why he had chosen their facility.

Jasper told him that his bank had been recommended to him by a friend who told him that they had an excellent reputation for higher interest rates, and they also had a fine vault for boxes.

Of course Mr. Egmont accepted the compliment about his bank and authenticated what he had heard was true.

Mr. Grant said that his father, some time ago,

purchased some bearer bonds. He felt that they were a safe bet and easier to pass on to him, his only son, than an account might be that would have to be scrutinized, and that would take a lot of time doing it.

Mr. Egmont, completely mesmerized with the thought of a large deposit, asked to hear more.

Jasper told him that he had ten, One Hundred Thousand dollar, bearer bonds and that he would like to have one cashed and put into his account, and the others to be held in a box that he intended to rent. Then he asked if that would that be possible?"

Having very few deposits of that type, Mr. Egmont welcomed him with open arms. He knew the value of having someone of means come into the community, and especially into his branch. He told him he was sure there would be no problem, and how pleased they were to have his account.

After the paper work was done, and while the bonds were being authenticated, Mr. Egmont, standing behind his desk, summoned his secretary and introduced her as Cathy. He then introduced Mr. Grant and explained that he had just opened an account with them and asked her to escort him to the vault and show him the security of their boxes? He also asked her to give him the brochures that outlined their procedures, safety precautions, and other things of interest, while he took care of the internal paper work.

Mr. Egmont, following the credit union procedures, contacted their main offices and advised his superior of the account being opened. Of course the officer at the main office congratulated his branch manager and told him that he would immediately verify that the gentleman, introduced as Mr. Grant, was indeed who he said that he was. In his checking of the information, he discovered that a man of the same name had recently passed away. While checking the social security numbers, he discovered that it was the same as the one Mr. Grant had just given to Mr. Egmont.

Immediately, Mr. Egmont paged his secretary. When she answered, he told her that she was needed immediately in her office, and to advise Mr. Grant he should wait there until she returned. When he was sure his secretary was safe, he alerted the credit union security officer, went to immediately take the man into custody and await the local police department.

John, the security officer, had worked for the branch office for several years. This was the first time anything like this had taken place, and it was just a few weeks before his retirement. He had been warned by his doctor, but did not advise his superiors, that due to his age, and his bad hip, he should not wait too long to leave the job that he so loved. Now, when he was needed most, he couldn't run, but had to limp his way to the vault, as quickly as he could. He was too late!

Mr. Grant feeling something was wrong, didn't wait as the secretary had requested, but hurriedly left the area. As he walked through the special metal detector he saw the limping security guard, and moving quickly, he ran through the lobby easily out distancing his adversary, and was able to reach his car and speed off.

CHAPTER 35

The research specialist at the police station was delighted to work with Frank and me with our microdot. It had been some time since he was given that kind of job and he dug into it with eager enthusiasm.

Killing time, we sat in the outer office of the lab, waiting to see the report. We discussed how Frank had been misjudged about the embezzlement in the past. He believed that Gertrude had stolen the money. She was a conniver of the first degree, and she had an insatiable desire for money. There was no way to prove it, and at the same time there was no definite proof that Frank had stolen it either. The fact was, she was an attractive young lady at the time, certainly that had been in her favor with an all-male jury helping to sway the jury, who she made believe she was being taken advantage of.

I asked him about Madge and him. It seemed to me they didn't fit together, then I apologized, and told him I was sorry, it was none of my business.

He told me he understood the question, and volunteered that when he got out of prison, he wasn't the same man he was when he went in. He was a lot harder, and with a lot fewer values. He didn't trust anyone and certainly didn't want to go back home.

Asking me to remember that he had been a heavy drinker before his conviction, he told me that the first chance he got, he went to the bar in that little town of Willow Point and drank up what few dollars he had after renting a flophouse room. Not having been around any women for those long years, he ended up in bed with the first woman that was willing, and was halfway attractive...that was Madge. She, taking advantage of the fact he landed a job as a car mechanic, moved in with him and the next thing he knew, she was pregnant with a little girl. He tried to raise the girl, but before he knew it, she was gone, and only 16 years old. It was at that time that he realized what a fool he had been. He quit drinking anything except for an occasional beer, quit talking like an uneducated fool, and decided to clean myself up. He said it wasn't easy.

He just finished with his story when the specialist told us that we would find his research interesting! He led us through the lab to his cubicle. He handed me the printed page from his desktop and explained it was a transcript of what they found on the microdot.

It read:

To whom it may concern,

Please notice that all papers have been authenticated and notarized by Elizabeth T. Betting, Notary, Guntersville, Alabama.

To Whom it May Concern:

Since my illness in 1991, my wife, Gertrude E.

(Gonzales) Dono, elected to misuse the funds from our company and divert them to a private account. Arrangements were made to handle this as a bookkeeping error covering up theft by Vice-President, Mr. Frank Dono, my brother. I have been under constant surveillance and imprisonment, since that time, by my wife, Gertrude E. Dono, and have not been in an official capacity to debunk this unfortunate situation. I have discovered that those fund distributions can be traced to the Bahama account of an unknown Madeline Kramer, AKA. Gertrude E. Dono. Account No. BN38254321.

Papers to document this information can be found at the Overland Bank and Trust, Box 212, Huntsville, Alabama, Box 83.

Sincerely,

John Dono

I don't know who was the most surprised, Frank or me, but Frank was the happiest. Then his smile faded as he asked if I any idea where the mandolin might be. I told him that the last I knew, Sean had purchased it from Ben Appleby.

If Sean had it, someone must have known and killed him for it...

The young research policeman was called to

another area. This left Frank and me alone. As soon we started our conversation again, the specialist returned and told us that there was something happening, right then, that had a reflection on the note he had just read to us! He suggested that we remain where we were.

Frank told me that he was overwhelmed with all of this information. It appeared that if we could find the mandolin, his life might suddenly be changed. His concern about Madge came to full bloom. He was sure that she was backward, un-educated, and had other faults, but he thought that she had a good heart. After all, she only raised her daughter the way that she had been raised and he admitted that he was worthless due to his drinking. He knew it was time for him to settle down some time ago, and he should have tried to get some kind of education for Madge that could have made a better life for them both.

The researcher returned and told us Sargent Johnson wanted to speak with us, especially Frank Dono. We left the room and followed the specialist to a small, private room where he was told Sargent Johnson would come very soon. In minutes he arrived with a story that would make a fat man dance.

He told Frank that a gentleman by the name of Grant, had tried to start a new account with some bearer bonds. They were issued by the Overland Bank and Trust Company in Huntsville. The gentleman claimed that he was given them by a relative, but they traced them the source, which happened to be the John Dono holding account.

CHAPTER 36

Gertrude had just sat down to an early dinner when Lori and I arrived to talk to her. She was unhappy to see us, but that was expected. We told her it was time that she knew who we were so we introduced ourselves as Bill Deavereau and Lori of the Deavereau Detective Agency. We explained that we had made several attempts at locating the mandolin and the banjo, but to no avail, and we were there to apologize to her for misleading her and several other people. Lori hated that part!

She belligerently suggested that we were only there to badger her about that banjo. Seeing that our apology was not being accepted, Lori, still irritated, told her that we weren't really there for only that purpose! She told her that we knew she sold it to Ben and then tried to buy it back, but that didn't work. We also knew that her brother in law, Frank, the man she railroaded to prison, was back in town and knew that she had tolerated Barry, and then discarded him like a piece of trash because he was too close to her husband, John!

Instrument of Death

How did she get all of that out in one breath?

Gertrude directed her question to Lori, asking that "Since we already had all of the answers, why were we there? That was when I noticed that she carried a beautiful ballpoint pen tucked into the front part of her dress, using the clasp to keep it from sliding inside.

I went on the offensive and told her that she had become the center of our investigation. I described how since Lori saw her last, as Judy Chillicothe, she called and baited her, and told her that she had the banjo. I asked her to tell me how she expected to pull that off.

She, in no uncertain terms, told me that it was none of my business.

I smiled my 'know it all smile' and told her I was making it my business, advising her that the day she threatened my partner, she made this investigation very personal. That wasn't bad enough, but then she tried to kidnap Lori. I told her she could thank her lucky stars that attempt failed!

She stared at me as though she was in control and told me she didn't have to listen to me and turning her head away from me, she shouted for Ruth to call the police! She shouted again asking if her daughter heard her and again ordering her to call the police. There was no answer. She had forgotten that her daughter had left. She tried to call Nathaniel, but we saw him leave with Barry so we knew she was there, alone. Gertrude told us she would just have to call the police herself.

I agreed she should. It probably a good idea because I thought they might be interested in the ballpoint pen attached to her blouse. She looked as though she had seen a ghost and asked what I meant.

She didn't know yet that the police knew she had made fake books which got her brother-in-law convicted of embezzlement.

Lori looked at me with that "are you nuts" look. Gertrude looked at me with fear and hatred. I felt like I had just struck a chord, and I didn't mean a banjo chord! Gertrude ran out of the room, then closed and locked the door. Never having been in any of the four rooms that adjoined the living room, neither of us had any idea where she might be headed. By the time Lori and I opened the locked door, Gertrude was gone!

Asked how I knew all of those things about her, I just smiled and told her, I learned them from Frank. The rest I made up!

My greatest fear, was that she would dispose of the pen attached to her blouse. I was certain it would have the D.N.A that would match both of the victims.

I pulled my cell phone and called Sergeant Johnson. I told him what had just happened and suggested an immediate call might be put out for her arrest. He agreed about the framing of Frank, but of murder? He sent out the BOLO based on the false testimony of Gertrude, years earlier that convicted

Frank Dono.

We still had some problems. Who was Mr. Grant and did he have the mandolin? If he had it, and was trying to cash the bonds by using a fictitious name...how did he get them? Did Gertrude stab the victims with her ballpoint pen? If she did, why did she do it?

Chapter 37

Lori had already gone, and now, Frank and I were left to handle what had to be done...neither of us knew for sure what that was. We finally decided that I should go back to my office and he to his motel in Arab. We agreed to keep in contact, should any new information arise. Madge awakened from her nap in the car, and they rode back to their place.

Lori was sitting at the desk when I returned to my office and told me she thought she had everything under control, because all at once, everything was so clear and right in front of us where it had been the whole time. I asked her what she thought we had "in front of us the whole time."

Right there in our own storage, she explained, we had the banjo. We assume by finding the banjo, the mandolin was going to appear like magic. It wasn't that way at all.

I asked what way was it then? She went to our storage closet where the instrument was, in its case. She grabbed it and carried it back to my desk. She told me to open the lid of the case and remove the banjo. I did.

Then she made the statement that we had examined the banjo and found the microdot. Again, I agreed.

Next, she pointed to the case and indicated that we didn't examine it, but assumed the bumps and groves in the velvet lining were age. She said that we could be very wrong and asked me if the bumps and ridges could be made by something under the lining. It was interesting watching 'Sherlock Holmes Junior' as she moved toward her goal of solving part of this case.

Paying no attention to me, she removed a penknife from my desk, opened the small blade, and inserted it into an area where the seam seemed to be a bit fragile. The seam popped open like magic, exposing a piece of paper. I was getting more excited now and less sarcastic and asked what was on the paper. Removing it carefully, she opened the folded paper inside. The top of the page had the Dono Investment letterhead. Under that was a date, and the heading read,

"Official Document – Corporate Exchange." She had just found the papers John Dono had written about in the paper at Police Headquarters.

Reading further, it said, the board of directors had officially acknowledged the following:

"In the event of the death of the Founder, President, and Chief Operating Officer, Mr. John Dono, it is his request, to which we all acknowledge is first and foremost in the company's interest, that Mr. Frank Dono be unfettered as the embezzler of the funds stolen by Gertrude Dono, and that he be nominated as the President and C.E.O. of said corporation, Dono Investments Incorporated. It is further directed, herein, that any living relatives of Mr. Frank Dono, be elected as Directors at Large for the duration of their lives to receive an equal amount yearly, as so indicated by Mr. Brent Simpson, Treasurer, at such a time as deemed necessary and proper.

Signed:

    John R. Dono, President, and C.E.O.

    William Buckley, Executive Vice President

    George Shelton; Director of Public Relations

    Brent Simpson; Treasurer"

The signatures of all of the executives necessary were there, including the signature of John himself. I was amazed at the document and told Lori that I had never seen anything like it before. Lori agreed and asked if I noticed that it was notarized and witnessed, then she asked if I thought Frank could handle this.

I told her that after all he had been through, it was going to take a bit of time, and first he would have to be sure his personal life was in order.

This guy has been through the mill. In his favor was a good education and knowledge of the company. All he had to do was worry about handling the money since his lovely sister in law had sold the company and only some of the assets remained, which I felt confident Frank could handle. But, we still had to find the mandolin!

We were both glad that Frank was innocent, and, not unhappy about the ditch Gertrude had dug for herself. I did wonder if Nathaniel and Ruth were involved in it or just unsuspecting bystanders.

We put the document in a manila envelope and left for the police station. Lori was pleased that this exonerated Frank from the embezzlement charge. I told her there was more information at the station, and it too, exonerated Frank. I told her it had come to light after she left the station, and with the excitement of her finding, I forgot to tell her everything.

Arriving at the station, document in hand, Sargent Johnson met us at the door. He asked why I had come back and I handed him the envelope. He asked what it was, and I told him it would be best if he looked at it himself. He agreed to do so. I asked him to tell Lori what else had transpired since she left the station earlier and he did. Lori was delighted with the information, and tears filled her eyes knowing that a lot of good was coming from this crazy-quilt case.

CHAPTER 38

After we left the station, Lori asked that since we had the banjo situation solved, what about the mandolin? Originally, we were to find the two instruments but we only had one in our possession! I told her that I might know where the mandolin was. She felt she had been in the dark because I had spent so much time, alone, with Frank. I explained to her that the idea had just come to me and had nothing to do with Frank and me spending time at the station without her and Madge. I told her it was a hunch, and I could be wrong.

Lori had her phone handy, so I asked her if google could give her the address of Mr. Falcone. She was astonished at my request, but complied with it and the phone did its google search giving us the information we asked for. Lori got moody and insisted that I was keeping her in the dark! She smacked me on the arm and gave me that pouty look.

I asked her if she remembered when we went to

the station with Frank and Madge. She looked irritably at me and said that of course she did, after all, it wasn't that long ago. Disregarding her answer, I related that she had become tired of waiting and left the station, taking my car and going back to the office, and I asked her if she remembered that. She sternly suggested that I stop asking her about her memory and tell her what we were doing.

I was just making sure we were on the same page. She gave me a look of approval, even a slight smile, then she reverted to that [eager to learn] partner I was so comfortable with, so I continued telling her what happened after she left, about the technician who read from the microdot that revealed how Gertrude E. (Gonzales) Dono diverted the missing funds to a private account, and how she set it up as a bookkeeping error to involve then Vice-President, Mr. Frank Dono. It also spelled out how John had been under constant surveillance by the police, and imprisoned by his wife who used several paid off psychiatrists who made it possible to show him to be unfit to handle his own affairs. That was why he could not rebuke her statement. He managed to trick her somehow, and he did some secret investigating on his own before writing his findings that would, someday exonerate his brother. He discovered the funds his wife had diverted, could be traced to the Bahama account of a Madeline Kramer, known also as, Gertrude E. Dono. Before he lost complete control of his own accounts, he diverted some cash into the $1.0 million in bearer bonds and saw to it they were hidden.

Lori, smiled and said that must have made Frank

a happy man. I told her that wasn't all.

Her smile dissipated and turned to an expression of curiosity when I told her Sargent Johnson, called Frank into his office to tell him that someone had tried to cash those very bearer bonds, and put the cash into a new account at the Credit Union branch.

Lori really felt she had been left out, until I explained that without her detective work regarding the Dono family and their relationship with Ben Appleby, a lot of the puzzle may have never come to fruition. She asked me to elaborate.

While she was watching over the Dono family it became more and more unlikely that they had anything to do with the location of the instruments. The actions of Mrs. Dono, with respect to her son and daughter sent up a red flag that she would do anything to keep them under close supervision. I asked myself why she would do that, being so greedy, if she could turn them loose from her monetary support.

She asked me, why would she?

The answer was simple. The old adage of keeping your enemies close but your friends (in this case children) closer was true. She could control their every movement, and as she had her husband, there would be no way for them to consider she might have done anything but be a poor wife. She kept them too busy to have the time to think about what had been happening during their father's illness.

Lori understood what I was saying, and equated it with how governments create activities that seem important and required constant tweaking, and during that time while the problems were being worked on, they, in turn, went in another direction without any questions.

Time was of the essence if we were to get ahead in this investigation. We had to work quickly if we were to divert any future problems that might become unsolvable. Lori was now up to date on the theory of Mrs. Dono, but there were other considerations that had to be made to find the missing violin, and identify the mysterious Mr. Grant.

I could have been wrong, but putting two and two together, I got four.

I asked her to consider that Sean and Jack may have worked together. Sean, in one of his conversations with Jack Falcone, mentioned his relationship to Frank Dono, and Jack, being a longtime resident, remembered the Dono Financials case. At one time, his bank had been involved with the Dono Financial Corporation too. He always believed that John was innocent of the crime he had been convicted of. At that time there was no mention of any instruments as this was a corporation crime, not a personal property one.

I suspected Sean may have sent a note to Madge, or called her on the phone after Barry's drunken babbling that night in Huntsville. It was possible that she was told Frank's wealthy brother was dead and some instruments valued at five or six thousand bucks were missing. She knew that Frank wanted his banjo because he talked about it often, but never mentioned its value.

Lori listened intently to my theory, occasionally asking a question or two about things like the relationship between Mary and her mother, and between Sean and his older sister, Madge. I had not mentioned those relationships, except for the one between Sean and Madge.

I suppose that we could assume that Sean was dating Mary just to get information, but even Madge would surely not have pushed that plan, knowing their relationship. I would rather assume that Sean talked to his boss, Jack Falcone. Taking an interest in this new mandolin revelation, Falcone could have decided to take a second look at the old records the bank kept regarding the distribution of Dono Corporation funds. If there was an accounting of money that wasn't found before, that money could have been hidden somewhere. The value is [in] the instruments, like [inside of] the instruments could have kept inflating Jack's imagination.

Lori, asked if I was telling her that all of the problems stemmed from Jack's imagination. I answered that I was willing to bet that the man, Mr. Grant, was really Jack Falcone.

Unbelieving, Lori stared at me, then she suggested that if I was staking our reputation on that, why did I tell the cops that Gertrude killed those people. Both she and Jack could have done it together, because she was on Gertrude's tail most of the time that these things took place. She asked if I didn't think I was getting carried away! Furthermore, she asked why would Jack kill Sean and Mary.

Mary just got caught in the crossfire. Sean was just protecting her, so he gave her free lodging. Remember, she wasn't lily white, and took advantage of a place to live. Remember, neither of them knew of the relationship which was hidden by the fact that she had legally dropped her last name. Unfortunately for her, Jack found her alone, in Sean's apartment while searching for the mandolin, but instead found a wildcat living there. She assumed he was a burglar and fought him with everything she had. Using the only weapon he had, he grabbed her and stabbed her in the neck with his pen.

Lori was still not convinced my theory would hold up, so I went further in my idea.

Supposing that he killed her and while searching through her things he found Sean's new address. After all, Mary had to have a way to contact him. Jack, had already killed once, so going to Sean's address to find the mandolin was no problem, until Sean came home to find him there and put up a fight. Jack, now very familiar with his pen weapon, used it again. He found the mandolin and assuming that it was the key to his future wealth, took it, and fled to his home.

Lori, still not buying the whole story, changed

the subject and asked me why did Gertrude tried to run away from us. She didn't have the instruments, and apparently she didn't kill anyone. Being as smart as she was, she had to be aware that the legal time had expired to do anything about her crime.

I didn't have an answer for that, other than maybe she had some tie-in to the case that I wasn't aware of, or maybe it was just too close to home for her to live with at that moment.

CHAPTER 39

We arrived at Jack Falcone's address given to us by google on the phone. I was surprised to find a nicely painted wood frame house with dark shutters covered with climbing Clematis. It was nice, and a relatively humble place right out of a fairy tale and didn't fit the man we were seeking. I knocked on the front door and Jack opened it.

He greeted me saying, Mr. Deavereau, I don't usually accept people at my home, isn't this something that could wait until tomorrow, during banking hours? I pushed on the door forcing it open. He asked what I thought I was doing and told me that this was his home and I had no right to…I cut his sentence short and told him that I knew he tried to pass himself off as Mr. Grant and suggested he had an expensive mandolin hidden there somewhere.

In an explosive move, Jack swung at me and

missed. I drove a punch to his neck and he collapsed like a wet rag!

Lori followed me in and cried out, asking what if I was wrong. I told her not to worry about it, and while he was out, we should check the room with the door closed. Lori did as I instructed and in a few seconds asked me to guess what she found.

I answered, "A mandolin!"

She came out of the room with the mandolin in its case, and told me that she also found a partially packed suitcase. As I had suspected, he was planning his escape.

The blare of a siren smashed our eardrums as a black and white pulled up in front of the place. Two officers moved to the front of the house and demanded that anyone inside come out now, peacefully, with their hands behind their heads.

Not wanting to be shot, we both complied. The officers told us to lay on the ground, although we protested. One of them stayed with us as the other entered the house to find Jack Falcone, lying on the floor, with blood trickling from his nose.

The officer inside yelled to his partner Sal, that he found Falcone, and then questioned who we were. I told them that we were P.I's and my identification was in my wallet. The officer rolled me onto my back and removed my billfold from my back pocket. He opened it and pulled out my driver's license; my P.I. license fell out at the same time. He called out that I was a P.I. and had a valid driver's license to back it up."

The other officer asked about Lori. She rolled over on her stomach, but had no identification on her. She cried out that they should look in the car, and told them that, men carry wallets, and ladies carry purses. The officer walked to the car, found her purse, and after dumping its contents onto the seat of the car, verified that she was a detective.

They let us get up and Lori straightened out her clothing while I put the identification back into my wallet. Another car pulled up, this time it was a black car with a large whip antennae. It was Johnson, and all he said to us was "You two again? Can't you stay out of trouble?"

I told him to give us some credit...after all, we did figure this out faster than he did! He told me that one day, my mouth was going to get me into trouble then he continued with old nonsense that they had to do things by the book, yaketty-yaketty-yak.

He looked at the uniforms and asked what they found. They described how they found the two detectives in the building, the man lying on the floor with his nose bleeding, and bags packed in the bedroom. By that time, a groggy Jack Falcone stood holding on to the doorframe, with an officer helping him stand shouting that he wanted to press charges against...

Johnson looked at Falcone disgustedly and

told him he had no doubt about that, then he told the officer to read him his rights and advise him that he was being arrested for forgery, fraud, and theft. and added, at least for starters.

Already knowing the answer, I had to ask if we could return the mandolin to its owner. I got the answer I had expected of sure you can right after the trial, it is evidence...I said with him, in an ongoing case!

CHAPTER 40

Both of us knew that the case was drawing to an end, but there were still some t's to be crossed. As we drove back to our office, Lori asked me what was going to happen to Madge. We knew that Madge had to be involved since I had seen Jack Falcone leaving her place, and they supposedly didn't know each other. We agreed to take a shot at her while all of this was going down and headed in the direction of the Dono's motel in Arab.

I knocked on the door and Frank answered it. He was glad to see us and we found Madge in the midst of packing. I asked where they were going. Frank told us that she was going back to their place in Willow Point. She felt she should go there and prepare for the move to Guntersville, since Frank had new responsibilities there. Lori wasn't about to let that happen knowing she was really going to try and disappear. She walked over to where Madge was packing and asked her point blank how she knew Jack Falcone. Shaken, Madge told her that it would be better if she didn't ask questions that were none of her business, and added that word, 'girlee.'

That was all it took. Lori had finally had it with her. She grabbed her by the shoulder and straightened her up from the bent-over position she had been in during the packing. Madge, expecting a punch, tried to pull away from her, but fell backward onto the bed screaming that the was going to kill that 'girlee'.

Frank tried to intervene and. I just stood there in awe of Lori's strength, and surprised at her lack of composure. She grabbed a handful of Madge's hair and shoved her head into the covers on the bed, while at the same time telling her that she knew Jack Falcone had been to this very room and she was who he had come to see. She went on to tell her that Jack was in custody, that he had attempted to cash in the bonds, and then she, voicing a guess, told her he was attempting to leave the country, alone.

Madge, not being one of the most intelligent ducks in the pond, became angry and insisted that Jack wouldn't do that to her.

Frank listened intently. Then, without fanfare, he picked up his cell phone, called the local police, and suggested they should come to the motel as a violent fight was taking place. I was concerned that Lori might be in trouble when they arrived, since she continued badgering Madge and Madge kept admitting more and more about her relationship with Jack, maneuvering her daughter into a fling with Sean, and how she had obtained information about the value of the instruments from Sean and Jack. Leaving nothing to the imagination, she gave Frank a reason to no longer believe her.

The police came, both Lori and Madge were arrested. I drove to the station after Madge was placed in the squad car, and met with Johnson. I asked him to release her into my custody. He agreed and for the first time during this whole case, he winked at me as the arrest was a big joke, at least for him. It brought back memories of a similar situation some time ago, but I won't go into that now.

Both of us felt that at last we were able to close the books on the instrument case. Barry would have to wait some time for the return of his beloved mandolin, but he did play with the jam group using his banjo and occasionally his guitar. He still hoped that one day he could replace his uncle's positon in the group with the beautiful, 1920 Gibson mandolin.

This was the longest two weeks of my life that I could remember. I found an apartment that fit my needs, with the approval of my partner, Lori. We thought this case would be an easy job, but, as usual, what started out to be simple became complex! There had been a lot of players, missing instruments, a couple of murders, a terrible family situation, but all in all, it was just another case.

Barry and his father were reunited. Frank couldn't get the company back because it was no longer in existence, but the million bucks in bearer bonds helped lift the weight of the company loss. Barry, on the other hand, opened his own club, and entertains nightly, along with his father playing there from time to time.

The Jam Session club still meets at Tony's place, of course with the new member, Ben, who never believed they would accept him. They even allow me to sit in from time to time, along with Barry when he has the time.

The Dono family has decided that after all of the problems that they created for themselves, that maybe they should start caring about someone else. They have founded a small charity that helps finance the rehabilitation of lost souls, those people that have no one, cared for no one, and don't want to get involved with anyone. It seemed to be the type of charity that they could appreciate with people they truly understood.

Ben's antique store is prospering. He did some advertising and I understand that he is now getting customers from as far away as Huntsville.

Jack Falcone was sentenced to life for the murders of Sean and Mary, and his associate, Madge will be very old before she is released for her part in the crimes that were committed. Frank divorced her before she was sentenced.

Gertrude Dono agreed to repay the amount

embezzled to the company officers, whose positions were created by Uncle John? She also had a lot of time to consider her actions while on parole each day wearing that lovely ankle bracelet that would be her exclusive jewelry for the next several months!

I never realized how devious Sean had been, or that Ben could be such a nice guy. Barry became a better musician than even he could imagine, and though this unique relationship became a constant companion of his cousin, Nathaniel.

There were several misguided judgements made, and no one fit into the slots Lori and I had them originally figured for.

Lori was manhandled, belittled, yelled at, and even teased. That one evening, which neither Lori nor I talk about, was interesting, at least what little I remember of it. While I'll never know for sure what took place that night, she is still my partner, my confidant, and my friend. We spend an evening out, from time to time. Once in a great while we talk about Joanne and the past, but not often. It is more fun talking with friends like Will and Linda, or going over to hear the old guy's jam sessions every once in a while. We go to Huntsville from time to time to see and listen to Frank and Barry on the stage, but still, one of our favorite things is a quiet evening, with good food at the old Rock House.

THE END

Other books by Thomas J. Ault:

My Name is Jake – No.3448700*

Jakes Animal Friends – No. 344912*

Jakes Travels – No.3455022*

Jakes Feather Friends – No 3455856*

Jakes World of Flowers –No. 3455875*

Jakes Nature Walk – No.3456079*

Jakes New Friends – No.3536736*

Jakes World For Kids –No. 3824359**

Every Hour Counts, or

    Gilbert the Clock No.3443266*

Moving West –No. 3686727*

The Incident – No.3482444*

Deavereau and the Napoleon Clock – 4210672*

Available at Amazon.com, and Createspace.com

*(numbers for createspace identification)

  **A compilation of all Jake books

Instrument of Death

Made in the USA
Columbia, SC
08 March 2022